Collateral Damage

And Other Stories

By

Bob Mustin

www.AMInkPublishing.com

ISBN: 978-0-9910330-1-0

Library of Congress Control Number: 2015949502

First Published by *AM Ink Publishing*, 6/2/2016

www.AMInkPublishing.com

AuthorMike Ink and its logo are trademarked by *AM Ink Publishing*.

Printed in the United States of America

TABLE OF CONTENTS

THE OFFERING

I can't tell you the precise moment I became aware of her. I could have caught a glimpse while listening to the tour guide talk of Tulum's history as we stood on the cliff there overlooking the sea. Or, earlier, before the tour began, the wind may have brought me the faintest scent of her perfume. All I can say for sure is that while squinting at Descending God's image over the entrance to his limerock temple, her presence beside me became palpable.

"I used to live here," she said, in a sudden rush of words. She squinted and pointed to the stone image. "I was his consort." Then she eyed me and smiled. "But that was, you know, many lifetimes after we were companions here. Human companions, that is." She ran a hand down one hip, brushed at her yellow sundress's skirt, and laughed, loudly enough to turn heads.

For some reason I haven't yet fathomed, I gave her a false name. Maybe I thought the name I gave her would appeal, make me more memorable than Nathan Ploegger, my all-too plebeian birth and surname.

She took my hand and as we walked she nattered on about her improbable relationship with this deity. Occasionally she'd turn and I'd feel her gaze probe me, as if she were plumbing my thoughts. After a while, her chatter tailed into self-conscious laughter. Then she took my elbow and turned me toward the tour group, now gathered just outside Tulum's gate.

We had an hour to eat and shop before the bus carried us back to Akumal, so we took a miniature train to a nearby shopping cluster. She suggested native food. I bought us beans and tortillas from a sidewalk vendor, and we sat on a nearby stone bench to eat. A young boy approached with an ancient Polaroid camera. He offered to take our picture for a dollar. We agreed.

As I pocketed the splotchy photo, she began another, over-long story. I've never been a fan of such one-sided talk; invariably I lose interest and tune out. But her voice enthralled. I listened, not so much to the content of her words, as to their music. She wasn't Mayan – her near-blonde, shoulder-length hair, much like my former girlfriend Susannah's, and her Philadelphia accent told me that much. But she was short, tanned a native brown, her nose faintly aquiline, and she had the same affability as the Indians I'd met since coming to the Yucatan. Strangely, I now remember her every word, every inflection, every expressive gesture.

"I came ashore two weeks ago today," she said.

Interesting. That was the same day I'd crossed from Belize into Mexico.

"I could see the structures from my cruise ship," she went on, "I could make out every detail, even though we were quite a distance away. They seemed so familiar, even from afar, you know?"

"I think a lot of people have that reaction," I replied. "Tulum seems to have an archetypal quality, maybe something about it that's buried in the collective unconscious."

She shrugged that off. "I was so attracted. I came here day after day. Had to drop off the cruise, I was so attracted. And you know what? Once I set foot here, the place began feeling, you know, very, very familiar. Every day it was something new. After a day or two, I could read the inscriptions. I could visualize structures no longer here, even the city's minutest details.

"Then one day I remembered being with the Olmecs. They were the ones who cleared the land and built the city. Well, it wasn't too long before Descending God came to be with us. He's from the planet Venus." She looked to the sea, and then again her eyes found mine. She giggled. "You don't believe me, do you?"

"I've read some of the legends. I realize it was a prevailing belief." I was beginning to see her as some sort of New Age dingbat. Still, with half of me swimming in smug cynicism, the other half kept whispering, Believe, you must believe. But why such inner jousting? I've always been purposeful, confident in my linear thinking. That is, until my father died and Susannah dumped me, both just weeks ago. But I'd left those ashes in Ohio.

"Oh, it was more than a legend, a belief," she replied. "I was here when he came."

"I see."

"At first, he was a pinpoint in the sky, like a ship on the horizon. He grew bigger and bigger, until we could make him out, and then he touched down." She snapped two delicate fingers. "Just like that."

"Ah."

"He walked straight to me. 'You're to be my wife,' he said. 'Isn't that lovely?' So we were married."

"And you lived happily ever after."

She looked away. "For a while. Then one day, we were walking just inside the gates. He told me he had to leave Zama. That was Tulum's name then. 'No,' I said, 'Please. Don't go!' But he did, on the next full moon. The same way he'd arrived, except in reverse. Into a point of light."

Her downcast expression seemed so genuine. "You must've been heartbroken," I said.

"You have no idea." A tear schussed down her cheek. "Then he told me, 'Don't worry, I'll return as often as I can, but difficult days are coming. I'm afraid I won't be able to come in this physical form until the end of that time. But whenever you're lonely or overwhelmed, you'll feel my nearness in the rain. You'll hear my voice in the wind.'"

We finished our lunch and browsed the souvenir shops, stopped to ask prices, the names of craftsmen, how they shaped their wares. I was amazed, not so much at her command of Spanish as she talked with vendors, as at her effortless lapses into the Mayan tongue, which I realized I could understand, too, but only in bits and pieces. We visited one last store, and there she saw me examining a knife carved from green stone. She took my arm.

"You like it, don't you?" she said. "I can tell."

"I'm not sure why, but I do."

"Of course you know. Come on, what attracted you?"

"It makes me feel, I don't know, odd." My eyes clouded.

"Sad?" she asked.

"Maybe. As if I lost something important once I saw it."

She nodded. "Or maybe you realize you're sensing something the people here have lost."

Her hand slipped to mine, squeezed it. She spoke to the shopkeeper at some length in Mayan, gesturing toward the knife as she bartered. Finally, the shopkeeper looked to me and nodded. She opened her shoulder bag and handed the man a wad of pesos.

She held the knife across both hands, raised it to eye level, and I took it. "It's a reproduction of a knife used in Descending God rituals," she said. "We're very lucky to have found it."

I thanked her and dropped the green shaft into my souvenir bag.

On the bus to Akumal, she told me more tales: the story of a man-child the god had given her. His name was Xupan, a renowned Mayan chieftain. A warrior, a poet, a seer. "He predicted the overthrow of the Olmecs," she said. "He initiated the great classical period of Mayan culture."

Our bus driver parked in front of my hotel, which was hers, too, as it turned out. She turned in her seat to take in the plaza and its people. "It was kind of like now. The Mayans were growing stronger as a people. Oh, I wish I had time to tell you all of it. It was such a magnificent time to be alive." We disembarked and chatted a few more minutes before she kissed my cheek and strolled into the lobby.

I lingered outside for a while, enjoying the afternoon breezes. Then, in the hallway to my room, I stopped. I didn't even know her name. I *had* to find out more about her. I walked the halls. No sign. And, of course, the desk clerk couldn't – or wouldn't – tell me anything.

For the next two nights I went sleepless. I tossed, rose, drank water, relived her stories, her mannerisms. The sound of her voice, the smell of her burnished skin, her hair. She became as alive in my awareness as the Yucatan itself.

Evening of the third night came. I was at my usual table in the hotel dining room. I had just turned a page of the local newspaper when I stopped in mid-bite and looked up. She stood before me, hands on hips, her face as radiant as the nearly full moon beyond the large window at the restaurant's far end. She shook a finger, pretended a pout. "I'm so angry," she said. "Where've you been?"

Without prompting, she sat, leaned forward, pressed her hand onto mine. Its warmth swept away any interest I might have had in the newspaper article I'd been reading. Then she reached for the menu our waiter offered and ordered a salad and tilapia with pilaf. We decided to split a carafe of chardonnay.

She looked down, tapped the paper. "What's this? You read Spanish?"

"It was a minor in college," I replied. "My mom's from New Mexico, and she insisted that Dad and I learn Spanish. She always wanted to move back there, but Dad's career wouldn't allow it." I looked away. "Dad, he died recently."

She gave me an odd smile, as if she'd just had some sort of epiphany. "Really," she said. "I'm so sorry. Is there anyone else in your life?"

"No. Not really."

We fell into small talk then. I eventually began giving her my views on Mexico, rather harsh ones, as you might expect. Drug gangs, and the killings, mostly near the U.S. border, but now spreading. The authoritarian leaders, who seemed to be relaxing their grip on the country a bit, but were nevertheless clamping a lid on movement, especially that of the poorer people. I tapped the paper and sneered. There was no mention of any of this in the local paper, I said. It was as if everything were hunky-dory here.

We sipped our wine. I told her of my concern for indigenous cultures, how modern life was shunting them aside, marginalizing their very lives. And of course that included the Mayan peoples. By then my talk must have seemed a rant. I went on about the dearth of meaning within my own life. She seemed to dwell on every word. As I talked, she filled my glass, then filled it again. And again. Finally my train of thought weakened and I fell silent.

"Are you all right?" she asked. "You've had a bit to drink."

For what seemed a moment, I closed my eyes. When I rubbed them open, she was gone. She'd scribbled a note on a paper napkin:

I'm sorry I had to leave before seeing you safely to your room. Let's meet here, at this table, tomorrow evening at seven. 'k?

Back in my room, I fell fully clothed into bed, expecting to swoon into unconsciousness. Instead, a deep foreboding took me. I couldn't breathe. I gasped and coughed, then rose and drank from the nearby pitcher. Panic overwhelmed me.

I scrabbled about in the room, searching for something, anything that might banish this awful feeling. The souvenir bag lay next to the bed. I reached in, probing, and closed about the stone knife. I cradled it in my palm, began to stroke the blade with a forefinger, as if sharpening it. The stone turned warm. The feeling of doom began to lift. I sighed with relief and, seconds later, I fell asleep.

I woke the next morning with not a scintilla of hangover. While sleep has always been for me part rest and part torment, that night it had been a complete, blissful unknowing. As I rose, I realized the knife had remained between my open palm and belly. For some reason, I began to laugh. I sat up, turned the blade to the morning light, inspected it wide-eyed, as a child might a new toy.

I breakfasted in-room and then pulled out a notebook I'd brought with me and began to journal. But all too soon, my thoughts returned to the woman. Frustrated, I stuffed the notebook into my suitcase, put on swim trunks and a tee, and left for the beach.

The day ripened to swelter, relieved only by intermittent breezes drifting inland from the bay. I walked along the wet sand for a long while. Noon passed. I ate at a cabana far down the beach, then swam for a while before returning to my room. The walk in tropic heat had depleted me, so I napped until after six and then showered. While rubbing dry in my terrycloth robe I happened to peer between the blind slats to the ocean. There she was – strolling at the water's edge. A man ran to her, stopped her. They talked, heatedly, it seemed. Then they hugged and walked together.

My face flushed and I began to pace. Was I jealous? Had I been indulging in some childlike, fantasy romance, simply because she'd shown me some attention? I dressed in fits and starts, selected one shirt, then another, and then changed trousers and shoes. During this unquiet process, I plotted ways to be alone with her, to touch her, to drown in the scent of her.

I stuffed in my shirttail, pulled on a seersucker sport coat, and near-ran to the restaurant. She hadn't yet arrived. The maître d' motioned me to my usual table. An envelope lay on a plate there. My name, or I should say the name I'd given her, had been printed on it in tiny, delicate letters. Inside, another note:

> I've been called away. Hate to stand
> you up, but it's a family obligation.
> Very complicated. So sorry. Me

I crumpled the note, threw it to the floor, and stalked from the restaurant. I swore, loudly. Screamed. Ran down the beach, then back, bellowing as might a deranged angel. I grew tired, my rants reduced to hoarse breathing. I staggered in one direction, then another. My feet turned leaden; I couldn't walk. Looking down, I realized I'd been walking in water, my Guccis soaked.

Normally this would've irritated to no end. I'm fastidious, one who would never ruin fine clothes through carelessness. But this time, my *faux pas* delighted – or more accurately, it excited. I waded deeper, the water creeping up my pant legs, the fabric cold against my calves, my knees, my thighs. I stopped only when the water's buoyancy made it difficult to tread the downward slope. Then a gust of wind came, and I thought I heard it whispering, "Are you nuts? Do you want to catch your death of cold?"

Back in the hotel room, I threw my soggy clothes to the floor, showered again, and fell asleep naked on the bed covers.

I rose with the morning sun. My obsession with the woman was upsetting me. I didn't want to think about the past I'd left in Ohio, the loneliness I'd soon be going back to there. So I began to mentally chronicle everything I'd experienced on the trip, as if there was a puzzle within it that I had to solve, something that might release me from my feeling of loss: my encounters with the woman, the places I'd visited, my feelings about everything that had transpired since I'd set foot on Mexican soil. But that only aggravated my obsession with the woman. I had to find her.

On impulse, I packed a bag, handed a note to the man at the desk to hold my mail, and I left Akumal. I didn't know where to go, but something told me she was still in Mexico. She hadn't meant to spurn me, I'd sensed that from the precise formation of her writing, the way she'd composed her words.

It occurred that my attraction to her wasn't romantic at all. She was beautiful, coy, even coquettish at times, the traits that had always drawn me to women. But I didn't want her physically, I simply wanted to talk to her, to find out more about her. If I could find her, maybe I'd come to understand what she was to me, the nature of our bizarre, offhand relationship.

I drove to Belize City, languished at the border as soldiers checked bags and vehicles. I searched faces. No sign of her going through customs. After two fruitless days, I returned to Mexico, stopped at a resort on the shores of a large lake. While lunching under its *palapa*, I showed the bartender the Polaroid.

He nodded. "Yes, she's been here."

My heart raced. "Do you know where she went? I have to find her."

"I see many faces, *señor*. I have a good memory, an excellent memory. But I cannot even tell you when she was here."

"Was she with a man?" I asked.

He shrugged. "Perhaps. I see so many faces."

I left, hopeful, drove the coast, the ocean always in my periphery, passed Akumal without slowing and entered Cancun, where I rented a room for the night. In early morning, I merged with the gaggles of tourists, searched among the natives selling souvenirs, peered at the peons bent to their various labors. I asked about her, showed the picture. Nothing. Then, late that night, in a beachfront cantina, I showed the picture to an old Indian woman.

"*Sí*," she said, nodding at the photo. "She had a drink here two nights ago." She sighed. "Alone. She was upset, I think, as if she was here trying to avoid something. Or someone. "

The next morning I approached a boy hawking small statues.

"Oh, yes, *señor*, I've seen her. She was a good tipper. She bought two small sandstone carvings and tipped me ten dollars American. Very nice. And beautiful, of course." He grinned. "You must be the gentleman she spoke of. I heard her mention him on her phone."

"No," I said. " Friends, that's all."

"I'm sorry, *señor*. Truly. Would you like to buy a carving?"

He reached in his knapsack, produced a statue made from molded concrete. I gave him a twenty. His coterie of friends followed him away, jabbering excitedly as he waved the money.

I searched all day. Nothing. I slept until eleven the next morning, a most fitful sleep. It took three cups of fine Mexican coffee to clear the cobwebs. *Chichén Itzá*, I thought – I haven't looked for her at the most sacred of Mayan sites.

I questioned tour guides there. In mid-afternoon, I showed the photo to a policeman, a tall, thin man of obvious Castilian descent, who spoke impeccable English.

"Yes," he said, "most definitely. She was here no more than ten minutes ago, in the company of a short Mayan man. Both were dressed well. Well enough to stand out in the crowd."

My pulse began to pound. I thanked him, darted through the growing crowd, searched faces. Nothing. Signs of her had cropped up everywhere I'd been; people had described her perfectly. Yet she was as elusive as the fog that settles over the Yucatan in the hours before dawn. Ephemeral, always just out of reach. I had to wonder: who – or what – was she? The silly airhead she seemed at first, exaggerated by my overactive imagination? And what was the feeling of cold apprehension that was slowly coming over me?

I returned to Akumal, parked at the hotel, and checked against all hope for a message.

"No, *señor*," the clerk said.

I stumbled to my room, frustrated, my nerves on edge. I paced. I threw wild, manic punches at empty air. I swore, albeit under my breath, so the people in the rooms next to mine wouldn't call hotel security.

Then I remembered the knife. I sat on bed's edge, began to stroke it. I let it slide to my chest, rubbed it across my abdomen. Doing this felt natural, and so calming. Finally, I fell to my pillow, still clasping the knife. Sleep came, a difficult, dream-tossed slumber.

In the morning, neither the knife nor a cup of instant coffee could expunge the despondency over my fruitless search for the woman. I have to refocus, I thought, I have to think about other things. I remembered a tiny library in Akumal. Maybe sitting for an hour or so and reading about local lore would calm me. The librarian there directed me to a small array of books. As I read, I heard soft laughter.

"Silly man," a woman's voice whispered. "What do you expect to find here?"

I spun, knocked several dusty volumes to the floor. Library patrons looked up, frowned. I grabbed my things and dashed out. A taxi sat idling a block away. A few shoppers wandered the street. If she'd been there, she'd negotiated a nimble getaway.

While walking to my car, I noticed a woman depart a small boutique. Her shoulder length hair was the same blonde. The same brown skin and petite build. Her yellow, floral-patterned dress looked a lot like the one she'd worn the day I met her at Tulum. I ran, caught up with her at the next corner. "Hey!" I exclaimed, laughing, "you won't get away this time."

The woman turned, gave me a quizzical look. I gasped. She was older, much older than I'd expected. I could tell now that broad streaks of gray corrupted her blonde hair. Her face had long since wrinkled beyond the masking ability of makeup. She was heavier in the hips, and her shoulders were slightly stooped. But her eyes were the same: clear, bright, penetrating.

"I'm sorry," I mumbled as I pulled out the photo. "I thought you were this woman."

She examined it, looked back and forth between the picture and me. "I look a little like her, I suppose." Then she frowned. "Actually, she looks a lot like my daughter, a great deal like her in fact. But the photo is of such poor quality, you know? We were vacationing together, but she's gone off on some adventure." A wistful smile. "She's such a difficult child, always complicating my life." She returned the photo.

I apologized again and plodded toward my car. How could I have mistaken this woman for her? This one seemed almost eerie, like a specter. I thought about that. I had been reading something about the Descending God legend just before I bolted from the library. What was it? Ah. Descending God had to be honored with a ritual sacrifice before the Mayan culture could rise again. I smirked, thinking about the clichéd sacrifice of a virgin. But, no, the depiction I'd read of this ritual seemed to indicate something else, some other form of ritual.

Then the smell of food hit me, and I realized I was hungry. I stopped at a sidewalk café, ordered a flagon of coffee and a pair of sweet rolls. As I ate, Descending God's ritual, it's odd, nebulous nature, kept haunting. I poured the flagon empty, stirred in a dollop of cream. Finally, it hit me. I knew what the ritual was all about, what there was about the knife that had saddened me.

I returned to my room, sat on the bed's edge, head in hands. No, it couldn't be true. This was simply a morbid thought hidden within my emotions, wrapped about the loss of my girlfriend and my father. All right, I thought, there's only one way to rid oneself of such unhealthy thoughts, you have to confront them head-on. I dressed, added a light jacket against the chill, placed the knife in my belt, finished packing, left a large tip each for the concierge and maid, and paid my hotel bill.

As I lumbered through the lobby with my bags, I glanced through the restaurant's glass doors. There she was, bent over the table I usually occupied, writing. She straightened, stuffed the note into an envelope, handed it to the waiter, and left by the rear door. I knew I couldn't force an encounter, so I loaded my car, then entered the restaurant and approached the maître d'.

"I saw a woman writing a note at my table," I said. "I'm sure the note you're holding is for me."

The maître d', a different one from all the other times I'd eaten here, eyed the knife in my belt and frowned. "Then may I see your identification?"

This exasperated. "Now, come on," I said, loudly. "I've eaten here every night." I pointed. "At that table."

He didn't reply; he only brushed a finger against a thumb to underscore his insistence on seeing my ID. I showed him my driver's license. As he inspected it, his frown creased deeper. "This says your name is Nathan Ploegger. The note is for someone else."

I nodded, somewhat frantically. "I gave her a different name when we first met, you see? I was feeling maybe a bit insecure that day and I wanted to impress her, she's very beautiful you know and I thought well maybe a more terse name would be more memorable that she'd remember me later and I've been looking for her all over Mexico these past few days and, well, I'm sure you see what I mean." I reached for the note.

Frowning, he snatched it away and motioned to the bartender, a large, barrel-chested man with arms as thick and solid as oak branches. "I'm sure you'll be fine after a good rest, Mr. Ploegger. This gentleman will help you to your room."

The barkeep clamped my arm with a powerful hand.

"All right," I said, "I'll leave. But I don't need to go to my room." What with seeing the woman and this difficulty over the note, I'd almost forgotten where I was going. "I'll just walk on the beach, I'm sure that'll help." I smiled, and the barkeep released me.

Outside, I breathed in the ocean's rich aroma, listened to the waves cough as they came in, watched them spread, ghostlike, and die against the sand. I walked the beach one last time, felt for the knife's hilt. Once again, touching it seemed to comfort me.

In the distance, I noticed a lone fisherman cast a line into the surf. Then, as if in a dream, I heard the woman's laughter. I peered past the angler, now silhouetted by the moon's translucent bubble. She emerged from the shadow of a pier, walked in my direction with another, a man. They approached and were about to pass when the woman stopped, tugged at the man's hand.

"Oh, look, it's my friend, you know, the one I told you about."

They neared, close enough for me to take in their features. The man was swarthy, with a broken-looking, downthrust nose. Obviously the man I'd seen her with days before. He was casually dressed, pants rolled up, barefoot, shoes in his hands.

After a moment, she walked to me, kissed my cheek, then bent, picked up a jot of sandy seaweed. "I left you a note," she said. "I'm, well, I'm going to be married. Again." She glanced toward the man. "It was rather sudden, I admit, and it was a difficult thing for me to accept. But it's the right thing, you know?"

I swallowed. "No, I don't know."

"I'm afraid it is. You could say it's destined. Under any other conditions, you and I –"

"Please, whoever you are, don't patronize."

"Anna," she said. "It's Anna." She giggled, turned away shyly, and then back with a deep, penetrating look. "You told me a fib, didn't you? You didn't tell me your real name."

"Yes, I'm sorry."

"It won't matter after tonight, but tell me. I have to know your name, too. It wouldn't be right, not knowing, given what you're about to do." She reached took my hand, rubbed the seaweed on it, her eyes never leaving mine.

I should've been angry, what with her trying to push me into this, but I wasn't. For some reason I couldn't be mad at her. I sighed. "It's Nathan."

"Is that what your mom and ex-girlfriend call you?"

"Nate. Everyone calls me Nate."

The man, who had been keeping a discreet distance, approached.

"This is Nate," she said.

I offered the seaweed-sopped hand, but he didn't take it; instead, his craggy features lifted into a smile.

"Nate," he said, filling that single syllable with a meaning and emotion I'd never known was there, "I'm so glad to meet you at last." He glanced to my waist. "I see you brought the knife."

I wanted to step away, to turn and run, but I couldn't. I'd become in some strange way frozen in place, as if I were separated from my body, no longer its master.

"You know about the sacrifice, then?" he said.

"That's why I'm here," I said, suddenly feeling loquacious. "I was in a rut at home, I guess, and I needed a change of scenery. I think I projected my own melancholy onto this Descending God myth, so I thought I'd come down here to the beach one last time and prove —"

He threw back his head and howled laughter, bent and slapped both thighs, a most uncharacteristic reaction for such a seemingly dignified man. "Myth!" He turned to Anna. "Did you hear that? He's calling it a myth now."

She shrugged, and I may have heard her choke off a sob, but it could have simply been the wave crashing behind her.

When he turned to me again, he seemed almost diaphanous, even though his face had caught the moon's full glow. "It's no myth, Nate. And, yes, that's why you're here. " He nodded toward the knife. "It's why you brought that with you. You're the offering we, the Mayan people, have been waiting for. The right lamb, so to speak."

My breath seemed to stop. I had to convince him I was here, not to take part in some sacrifice, but to shed the gloomy state I'd projected onto the ancient legend.

"Your sort," he said, "your people, they once had their own myths, as you call them, but they've forgotten them. These stories were promises, part of your perpetuity as a race, as this one is ours. Your people were once a lot like us, you know. But now you've all become so, well, so unhinged from the earth."

"I haven't!" I blurted. "I'm sympathetic. I know how the Mayans have had their culture submerged –"

"And that's why you've volunteered," he said. "That's why you've offered yourself."

"But I haven't –"

"You have," he said. "You have."

Something in the way he said those two, final words spoke volumes. It was as if there was no riposte left to offer. I bowed my head and nodded.

I felt his hand on my shoulder, although it seemed all but weightless.

"Good, Nate. Good. I knew you'd come around. We'll wait here, just a few feet away, give you room enough to do what you have to do."

They moved silently into the darkness. I know they're still there, though, I can feel their presence. Mom and Susannah will read about this, and I'll no doubt seem a pathetic wretch, a solitary misanthrope, to be pitied, in retrospect perhaps even feared. That's the way I'd feel, too, were I not ensnared in this drama I seem to have chosen, yet paradoxically, have had thrust on me. Maybe the gloom I've been feeling reaches far deeper than I thought. Maybe trying to dispose of it by coming to Mexico, and then by naysaying a local myth, maybe they're only symptoms of a darkness much wider and deeper than my own. Maybe this darkness belongs to all men, maybe even to the earth itself.

Whatever the true rationalization, it's as Anna said, it's destined. I know that now.

COMPLEMENTARITIES

Complementarity - a situation of physics in which different observations of a particular phenomenon are incompatible.

Jimmy Sheephorn was my only true friend. Even so, I still have to consider him odd. Part of it was physical: his six-seven height, the binocular glasses that summoned vertigo when his flitting eyes happened to meet mine, the unkempt black hair that hung to his hunched shoulders, the concave chest, the emaciated waist and gangly legs. Prior to college, his front teeth had grown a luminescent green tinge, and he always seemed to move about within a cone of falling dandruff. This latter pair of traits ended, though, during his second year at the University of Tennessee with the emergence of his new girlfriend, Juanita. I was never sure why she was drawn to Jimmy, but you can't argue with fate, I suppose. Anyway, this extremely attractive Honduran exchange student sent him packing to a dentist for a complete re-do. Then she bought a gargantuan supply of anti-dandruff shampoo, and every night she washed his hair in the old lion-footed tub of their seedy Knoxville rooming house apartment.

But now, as I consider Jimmy yet again, what I remember as oddness wasn't his appearance, or anything he did or said. He was a smart guy, wasn't a social goofball, and he'd always been a loyal, considerate friend. Rather it was, I think, events Jimmy had little part in that created an aura of oddness about him. So why do I even mention him at this point of my life? After all, he's been dead for some three decades. It's just that I keep thinking about that terrible, calamitous day he died, and remorse for my part in certain events involving Jimmy seems to have seeped into those thoughts. At any rate, until yesterday I'd never been able to reconcile the eerie feeling that he's still here. Maybe, I think now, the phenomenon we call death isn't what it seems; maybe life goes on in ways we find hard to accept. And that only becomes clearer when I think about Juanita, beginning with the day she left him.

I knocked on their rooming house door late that morning, expecting him to bellow out his usual, affable,

"Who is it, and whaddya want?" That thunderstorm roar would sometimes have an edge, complemented by Juanita's lisping Spanish invectives – another ninety-decibel argument in full force. And so I knew something was up when his simple "Yeah?" thudded against the front door like the bass lines from those old electrostatic stereo speakers of his.

I tried the door. Unlocked. Juanita always insisted on locked doors in that druggie-infested neighborhood. I pushed it open, just enough to stick my head in and announce myself.

"C'mon in," he called out in a fatalistic tone I'd never heard from him before, "I'm taking a dump."

I edged in and looked around. Most of the furniture was gone – and by furniture I mean a quartet of beanbag chairs. Also gone were the many pieces of pottery, woodcarvings, and porcelain figures Juanita had bought to fill spaces between the books and record albums on Jimmy's plank-and-cinderblock shelves. All that remained in the way of furniture, other than the half-empty shelves, was the room's centerpiece, a water-stained telephone cable spool Jimmy and I had wrestled up two flights of stairs a year or so earlier. An oilcloth cover now clung to it, one end on the floor like the bridal train

Juanita had always imagined wearing as she walked a church aisle to Jimmy. She'd bought it to cover up beer and wine spills, and a lattice of roach burns from the pot parties they threw, conclaves that could go on for a whole weekend. The heat had been turned down, more evidence of Juanita's absence.

"C'mon down the hall," he called out, "I don't feel much like yelling."

A short, dark, high-ceilinged hallway opened on either side to two bedrooms, one of which Jimmy called the Passion Pit, an almost bare room, a blue bulb dangling from one of those rope-like, early 1900s light cords, and a mattress at the room's center, covered with a yellowed and stained flannel sheet. There, if gloriously stoned and sexually inspired, you and your partner could strip down and swap fluids. The hall ended at the bathroom door and, given some awareness of the scent Jimmy's offal could emit, and what with a faint aroma of Michoacán reefer coming from the toilet area, I decided to stop halfway down.

"Juanita left, huh?"

A crackle-pop, followed by a revived essence of reefer. "Looks like. What's up?"

I couldn't help smiling at his feigned indifference. Then the gurgle of a toilet flushing. I hurriedly backtracked to the front room before the bathroom door opened full blast to his emanations.

Jimmy appeared, stuffing his shirt into his jeans in haphazard pleats, the joint dangling from one side of his mouth. He twisted his baggy jeans to and fro, licked his fingers, ran them through his hair, and then he proffered the joint. Remembering where it had just been, I declined. Then he waggled a finger toward the postage stamp-sized kitchen, and I took a seat on one of the three metal dinette chairs crammed against the wall opposite an ancient gas stove while he set his coffee pot to perking. Coffee made, he poured for us both, pulled away the chair next to me, turned it and sat, arms dangling over the backrest's cracked, floral-patterned Naugahyde.

His head slumped toward the chair's backrest. "Didn't see it coming, man."

I knew that wasn't so, given their constant fights and his slowly developing pushback against Juanita's fiery nature. "It's over, then?"

"I had hoped we could continue seeing one another," he said, "and, okay, maybe not exclusively. You know how she is, though, she just said it was over, it was too much, we were like fire and gasoline. In *every* way, including in the sack." A toothy grin that failed to disguise his sadness. "As if that's a bad thing."

I raised my coffee cup to my lips in case the sense of guilt I was feeling over his loss had etched itself into my expression. "I hate it, Jimmy. I'm really sorry. I guess I didn't see it coming, either." True, I hadn't been certain that she was leaving, at least on that particular day, but now that the cat was out of the bag, I knew where she'd gone — she'd moved in with a female acquaintance of mine.

How did I know this? Juanita and I had been part-time lovers for well over a year. I'd wake in the early morning hours, Juanita banging at the door to my natty little cross-town apartment, her blouse half buttoned, skirt or jeans twisted and awry, evidence of her hurried dressing. She'd throw herself at me, kissing every inch of bare skin she could get to. The first time that happened, I shoved her away. "What are you doing?" I demanded, looking past her to the parking lot. "Is Jimmy with you?"

"He is a bastard!" she yelled. "I do so much for him and he ignores me!"

My next-door neighbor's door creaked open, and I heard muttered cursing. I put a hand over Juanita's mouth, pulled her in, shut and locked the door. She seized my hand, began licking my fingers, and pressed her hips into me. "I don't love him," she whispered hoarsely. "I never did. It's you, Frankie, it's you I want. I've always wanted you."

How was I supposed to respond to that? We were naked in seconds, and she wrapped her slender, ivory legs around me.

"Take me to your bed," she whispered, "I want you, Frankie, I want *all* of you."

Boy. Wow. To say she was passionate is the grossest understatement. We made love in every way I'd ever imagined over my then-twenty years, and in a couple I hadn't yet conceived of. We fell asleep for a while, and then she woke me for more, and we went at it again until the night sky faded from a lubricious ebony to languid gray. Finally, I rolled away. She swung a leg over me, straddled me, and kissed me, ever so tenderly.

"You like Juanita, no?"

I slapped her fanny and smiled. "You bet."

"As much as you like Jimmy?"

"Jimmy?"

"Jimmy, *sí*."

I remember cringing a bit at the uncomfortable implication buried in her faulty English. "It's not the same thing, Juanita," I explained. "We're pals, Jimmy and I, we don't have this big, you know, emotional connection, at least not like the two of you have."

A most serious look took her, and she waggled a finger between us. "No, no, no, Frankie, you have been these pals since you were *niños*, isn't that so?"

True. We'd grown up in the same Atlanta neighborhood. I'd gone to private schools, he to the public ones, but we'd played on the same Little League team, and then later, despite our eventual ten-inch disparity in height, we'd played basketball together, rec leagues and all that. And it was true that I had turned down Rutgers for U.T. and its law school, somewhat fearful I think now, of going to college away from home, where I wouldn't know a single soul. Jimmy had already been awarded a scholarship to U.T., his curriculum mathematics, with an eye to advanced degrees in nuclear physics and, to the extent that I followed him there, I suppose we did have a fairly close fraternal attachment. So I nodded yes to Juanita's question.

She slapped my chest, as if my admission had proved some highly debatable point. "You see?" she said.

"You see, Frankie? You have been *amigos* for such a long time." Her head dropped and she sighed into my chest. "Jimmy and I, we have been close for only these past year." She sat up and shook her head, a sad expression distorting her beautiful face. "My parents, they give me so much grief about Jimmy. They say *los Americanos,* like Jimmy, they are not good men, not like the Catholic boys in Honduras."

I had to smile at her childish view of things. Despite my post-coital dullness, I realized I shouldn't compound her confusion by reminding her that I was American, too, and so I said, "I think you're a lot closer to Jimmy than I'll ever be."

Her head snapped up, green eyes wide. "Do you think so, Frankie? Do you really think so?"

I brushed her long brown hair away so I could better take in her bright-eyed, innocent expression. "I know so. You're all he talks about when we're not discussing academics. No, absolutely, Juanita. He's had girlfriends before, but they never had that much of a hold on him. Not like you have."

She brightened even more. "This is true? Even if I am working my way through U.T. with bookkeeping in the dean's office? I'm just a student of biology, you know, the genetics, and Jimmy's going to be a famous atom scientist."

"Doesn't matter," I said. "Honduras might be class conscious, but here such things don't matter. People get together romantically from all walks of life. At any rate, I know for sure that cultural differences don't matter to Jimmy."

She gasped as an aha moment registered, and she leaped from the bed. "I must shower, and then I will go home to Jimmy," she called out over one shoulder. "I will tell him he's not such a bastard for ignoring me, that I know he loves me so, so much!"

She showered quickly, dried her hair, and I watched her glide about, naked in the gossamer moonlight as she recouped her strewn-about clothes. Dressed once more, tucked and buttoned primly this time, she bent, kissed me, and dashed away.

The same scenario played out at irregular intervals for months. A few times, insecurity over her relationship with Jimmy at a breaking point, she'd broach the subject of moving in with me. I always said no, emphatically. Why? she'd ask. Jimmy is such a bastard. He ignores me. I am beautiful, no? Sure, I would say, of course you are. But you have to understand, he has to maintain his grades at a certain level in order to keep his scholarship. There's a lot of pressure on him, and I'm sure as soon as this series of tests is over you'll have his undivided attention. Such assurances would satisfy her for the most part, but I could tell that something was eroding in their relationship, something Jimmy's undivided attention could never repair. She began asking me if I knew another woman, a good woman, someone she could feel comfortable rooming with.

I did know such a woman, a Spanish major with whom I'd been having a minor fling. Her composure and calming ways would probably prove the right counterpoint to Juanita's explosive nature, so I mentioned her to Juanita a couple of times. At that point, and at my request, Juanita had begun calling before she came over, and during one such call in late afternoon, I told her I'd like her to meet Lucinda.

"Who?" she screeched into the pay phone receiver. "Who is this woman?"

"Take it easy, Juanita, it's just the woman I told you about, remember? The one you might want to room with? I thought you should meet her."

Silence, and then: "Oh." She hung up.

So I got Lucinda on the horn and told her what was up. She'd had an emergency appendectomy a couple of months before, and while she was faithfully making payments on her medical bills, she was in a bit of a bind, so she was open to a roommate, had already interviewed a couple of women toward that end. This time Juanita's knock was timid. Before I could get up to answer, the door creaked open and she stuck her head in, saucer-eyed and wary – the little girl within her fully exposed. But she and Lucinda took to one another immediately, and they even hugged as Lucinda's half-hour visit ended.

I hadn't expected any lovemaking that afternoon; actually, I was beginning to tire of our grudge-fuck trysts, Juanita always going home to Jimmy as soon as her anger had cooled. But as soon as the door closed behind Lucinda, she jumped me. We made love in the living room, then in bed, then, hungry, we ate fruit, and we did it on the kitchen table. And then in the shower. This time she didn't go home to Jimmy until the next morning, when I left for my classes. I knew the end was near for her and Jimmy, and I began to reconsider my refusals to her move-in overtures. But I was grappling with studies, too, and I couldn't face the possibility of her storming out of our place and running to someone else – maybe even Jimmy. Or maybe Walt.

Jimmy had made a friend, a student-teacher of freshman trigonometry, a guy named Walt, who made a few extra bucks working in a photography shop on the north side of the campus. Jimmy and I had lunch one breezy spring day, and afterwards we decided to take a walk. We ended up at the camera shop, and he introduced me to Walt. Walt and I hit it off really well, and I found that gratifying because by then it was our senior year at U.T. and I still didn't have anyone other than Jimmy that I could consider a true friend.

"Nice guy, huh?" said Jimmy, as we strolled toward our classes. I agreed, and was about to get downright effusive about it when Jimmy said, "I've been cooking up something between him and Juanita."

I stopped. Jimmy turned and gave me a silent chuckle, a playful expression on his face, but the sort of playfulness that could hurt someone else if not handled just right. Anger exploded in me over his pronouncement. Oh, I didn't say anything immediately, but I know it showed. He cocked his head to the left, closed one eye, and took me in, as if through a telescope. "You jealous, Francis?" he asked. (He called me that instead of Frankie or Frank when there was something of an edge between us.)

"Jealous?" I sputtered.

"Yeah, jealous. Look, I've seen how you look at her, and I figure you've got a serious case of worship-from-afar. I'm not an idiot. I can tell you've gone all candy-ass over her, but what she needs is a friend, someone who can talk her down from all those we're-over moments between her and me. So, since I figure you can't be that sort of friend, Walt gets the nod."

I just shook my head and clenched my fists, words unable to escape my too-dry mouth.

He set one of his foot-long paws on my shoulder. "I hope you don't mind my doing this." Then a sad, faraway look. "I've had to realize that despite how I feel about her, she's not long-term material, you know? She's going back to Honduras after graduation, and having that overbearing mother and dominating father around, well, she won't need me to add to her burdens. And then there's this guy her parents have promised her to, some electrical engineer, as I understand it. Anyway, those traditional, Catholic families like Juanita's? They look down on us secular Yanks. So despite my feelings, I've had to admit that she and I are just a convenience." A long, whistled sigh. "Best I can do is supply her with a back-up support system until she's out of my sphere of influence. End of story."

No, I told him, despite all your rationalizations, no! How could you have been living with a woman like Juanita all this time, a woman with such passion, and decide now that the whole thing was a mere convenience? I certainly couldn't have been that cavalier about her, and besides, her emotional hold on me had always seemed as tenuous as a feather tickle.

He squeezed my shoulder. "That's the difference between you and me, Francis. For someone who wants to be a lawyer, you sure don't trust your ability to reason through things."

That was true, although it wasn't easy to admit. We were already role-playing in one of my pre-law classes, debating cases out of law books before one another, and while I was able to arouse my classmates' emotions in those wordy duels, I never made As from them. We're into gray areas with these cases, Mister Ventura, the professor would lecture. Gray areas, you understand? You may sway a jury with your histrionics, but how much case law will you make? No, you need to learn to think on your feet. And you need to use reason, Mister Ventura, reason!

So I decided to test my reasoning abilities in that moment with Jimmy. "All right," I blurted, "let's say that you're right, that it's not in the cards for the two of you. So, if you're planning to dump her eventually anyway, and even if she is going to return to Honduras, why don't you push her my way? I could use some real romance in my life."

His look faded to bemusement, but with an uncharacteristically hard edge. "She'd eat you alive, Francis," he said. "It'd be like living with a hungry she-tiger. You'd be a basket case in a couple of months. I wouldn't want that to happen to you."

There's nothing like an unwelcome personal truth to knock the sand out of an argument, so I stalked off. But over the next two days, having given what Jimmy said a lot of thought and yet unwilling to let go of Juanita, I began showing up at Walt's shop, ostensibly shopping for a good camera, but really trying to get to know the guy. Okay, what was I trying to prove? That I could cuckold him, too, in some sort of weird, four-way sex-fest, with Juanita at its center? But despite what Jimmy was about to set into motion, Walt and I continued to get on nicely. We had lunch a couple of times, and even double dated once, me with Lucinda, he with some irritable redhead fix-up. On the way back to my place, as Lucinda and I chatted, I mentioned that Walt had negotiated the redhead's irascibility with great skill.

For a while she didn't say anything. I kept glancing at her, noting a look of amusement in the glow from the dash's light. "I guess you figured out," she said, "that Walt and I are an on-again-off-again item."

I hadn't figured anything of the sort. "Really? I don't –"

She patted my arm. "It's all right, Frankie. It's just been a casual thing, no strings, you know?"

"Okay," I mumbled.

She scooted over, snuggled into me, her head on my shoulder. Then she reached up and kissed my cheek. "If you didn't have such a thing for Juanita, I think you and I could get serious."

Well, that certainly took me by surprise. How could she have possibly known about Juanita and me? A gas station loomed through the late night fog, and I pulled up at one of the three pumps. Instead of getting out, I turned to her.

She sighed and, a hand over her mouth, she gave me an impish look. "I just have to tell you this story."

A story. Great. Just what I wanted from her. I held up a finger, beckoning her to wait. I got out, re-fueled, and paid. "Okay," I sighed as I climbed back in, "a story."

She nodded. "It was my freshman year, the day before spring break. I had thought Spanish would be a crip curriculum, but my high school version of it went out the window after the first month. For the life of me, I just couldn't gain fluency with it, not the way the others did. So I made an appointment to see my advisor, a Ms. Appleton, who was handling a lot of insecure students like me. Well, six of us were waiting that afternoon, and she was spending a lot of time with each of those ahead of me, so she was running behind. I was about to bag the meeting and go to my next class when this tall, well built, good-looking guy walked up."

"Walt?" I said, my tone pleading for it not to be so.

"Walt, yes, of course," she said. "I was upset about the wait taking so long, and he was awfully cute, and I think I was feeling more than a little needy at the time, so I started flirting with him. He later told me he really hadn't needed to see Ms. Appleton, he'd seen me putting my name on her sign-up list and he'd signed up, too, so he could meet me. Anyway, you know Walt, he took my craziness in stride, made me feel as if we'd known one another for a million years, and before I knew it, the door opened to Ms. Appleton.

"She's such a good counselor, you know? She listened to me for a solid fifteen minutes and then pointed out that a high school valedictorian such as myself would have all sorts of competition in college, especially in a Spanish curriculum, in which a lot of students probably spoke the language at home. That a B-minus grade point wasn't that bad, really, that if I knuckled down, went to the language lab more, then maybe I'd be able to hold my head high at grading time. So when I emerged from her office, I was smiling and ready to take on Spanish with renewed fervor.

"'You going in now?' I asked Walt. Mrs. Appleton was waiting and smiling, but he shook his head. He told her he had some things to think about and he'd come back later if he needed her. She smiled that motherly smile of hers and motioned the next student in. Walt leaned to my ear and said, 'Let's get outta here.' 'Where to, gumshoe?' I asked, you know, in that whimsical way of mine. 'West Virginia,' he whispered, as if we were about to become involved in some sort of conspiracy. He asked if I had camping gear, and I told him I did, so we hurried to my place so I could pack. He had his stuff in his VW microbus already, and we took off at breakneck speed, the old van rattling and lurching, and we found the campsite he was looking for just after nightfall. Walt built a fire and we cooked and ate and then sat there listening to the quiet."

She had set her hands on my arm, and now she squeezed hard with both. I wasn't particularly fired up to hear the rest of this story about her and Walt, who was probably already dabbling in Juanita's catalog of sexual pleasuring, not to mention, via this story, about to become Lucinda's lover. She was waiting for a prompt from me so she could go on with her tale, and I suddenly realized she was about to reveal something truly intimate. I figured maybe she really was the friend and lover I needed, the thing Jimmy had in Juanita on a good day, that this was something she wanted to get off her chest, that it was an opening to a next step between us, so I cleared my throat and said, "You're certainly making this road trip sound mysterious."

This was the best cue I could have come up with. She laughed loudly. "Well, I guess I meant it to be. I wanted you to have the same sense of foreboding I'd had as we drove those two hundred miles, listening to his eight track tapes." A sigh. "Creedence Clearwater was his favorite band, probably still is, and I hadn't really gotten their music, you know? But driving along those mountain roads like a couple of maniacs, I got it, really got it. Oh, he played some other stuff, too, but Creedence was it for us. Choogling. We just kept on choogling."

She leaned back, her eyes closed, and started a rhythmic head-bobbing to some silent beat. That went on for a minute or two and then she gave me a big, luminous grin. "Anyway, I was so caught up in the moment, listening to his music, digging the scenery, that I had completely forgotten to ask him what we were going to West Virginia for. So we were sitting together before the fire, taking hits from a bottle of tequila, and it finally slammed me like a bug on a windshield that he'd taken me on this trip for a purpose, a special purpose. I asked what was up. 'You like to live dangerously?' he asked. Answering questions with questions was one of my bugaboos, still is – keep that in mind for the future, Frankie – so I shrugged. Just shrugged. He eyed me as if he didn't know how to take me, and then he took another hit from the tequila and said, 'We have some choices to make, Luce, so I'm gonna leave it up to you.' 'What choices?' I said. 'You're scaring me, Walt.' Well, by that time we were kind of drunk, neck deep in one of those cold weather tequila highs, and I decided I really didn't mind that he wouldn't answer me. I kissed him. Then we – well, I know you don't want to hear the gory details.

"Anyway, the next morning, after he'd made a super omelet and we'd eaten it with some grilled ham and skillet bread, a guy drove up in a big flatbed truck with some strange-looking contraptions on the trailer. Walt got up and talked to the guy for a couple of minutes and then he tugged at one of the contraptions, which looked a little like an origami bird. They talked some more, probably negotiating a price or some such, and Walt came back and said, 'Your choice, babe. Hang gliding or a parachute jump?' He had to explain hang gliding to me, it was a new thing, still is, so I looked left and right. 'Where, Walt?' I asked, 'where would we do that?' He pointed back up the road from our camping spot and he crooked a finger northward. 'New River Bridge,' he said. 'C'mon.' So we drove to the bridge, the flatbed following us, and we parked off to one side of the gorge. What a sight that was! Something like nine hundred feet above the river. The bridge was completed but not yet open to traffic, so we just stood there for a while listening to the wind and taking in the view. 'All right,' Walt said, 'you've dawdled

long enough. I'm thinking you should just parachute off.'
On impulse I said, 'No, let's do the hang gliding thing.' So
he and the other guy took a while to explain how to get
into the harness. I crawled into it with their help and they
checked all the lines and harness straps and snaps. Walt
told me I'd drop like a rock for a couple of seconds, and
then the wind would catch the glider's wings and I could
glide about, maybe even soar on the updrafts."

"So you did it," I said, impatient now, and really
not wanting to have her story drawn out any further, since
it was clear that Walt had ended up being more than a
sports guru to her. "And you liked it."

She looked at me rather strangely, and for a
moment she didn't speak. Then a rapturous smile. "I did
do it, Frankie, and I loved it! But don't you see? It was a
risk, a really big one. I came to realize in that moment that
you can only gain from life what you're willing to risk. The
bigger the risk, the bigger the payoff. I want you to think
about that. Play it safe pining for Juanita, or maybe soaring
with me."

Well, she might as well have been talking to the
man in the moon. I wasn't a risk taker then and I'm not
now. That's why, after four years of criminal law litigation,
dealing with my dope-smoking, gambling, exotic dancer-

chasing law partners in Atlanta, not to mention the judges, who took bribes or were too drunk in court to care about the cases, I went back to school in a business administration curriculum and have been teaching business law in a suburban Atlanta community college. Still, I have had my moments, one of them a really, really traumatic deal involving Jimmy, the one I alluded to earlier.

That moment occurred back in 1984, April twenty-seventh. A warm Friday. I'd departed Atlanta for Knoxville, where Jimmy was teaching math to high schoolers. It was a mission thing for him, this teaching. He'd decided he could do more good teaching underprivileged kids than he ever could in the rarefied arena of high-energy particle physics. So anyway, we were going to have lunch near the school and then light out for a weekend of hiking. But first I wanted to sit in on his ten a.m. calculus class, see what the teaching end of school was all about, and he was cool with that. But I'd had a flat on the Interstate and, teeth chattering and knees waggling as cars and semis whooshed by less than an arm's length from me, it took over an hour to change the tire. Then I sat behind the wheel for another fifteen minutes, still shaking as I waited for an opening in the traffic.

By the time I found a parking place a block from the school, noon had come and kids were flooding the school grounds, some to eat their lunch on the terraced campus lawn, others racing for their cars. I was about to cross the broad avenue separating me from the school when I noticed Jimmy waiting for me at the corner walkway, a head taller than all the mostly black kids swirling about him. Just as I was about to cross, the light turned red. I decided to cross anyway, but Jimmy waved and shook his head, so I waited. A few seconds later, a primer-gray Camaro pulled up in front of Jimmy, and one of the boys in the car yelled something and started waggling an object in Jimmy's direction.

A gun! Suddenly the kids started racing away, as if fragments cast from an exploding bomb. I took off, dodging through traffic toward Jimmy and the car. Almost there, a pop-pop-pop echoed through the oaks lining the broad street. One kid stood frozen in place in front of Jimmy, and as the pops sounded, the kid's head flew back. Jimmy grabbed the boy, turned protectively, and then Jimmy's arms flew out, as if he were about to fly. He and the kid fell apart and lay unmoving on the sidewalk. The guy with the gun was a brawny sort, and I don't know why, since I've always been a wimp when it comes to fighting, but I made a grab for the gun. The brawny kid and his driver were just sitting there looking at Jimmy and the fallen boy, as if transfixed by their crime. The shooter's hand had gone slack, and I jerked the gun from him. They swore at me, and then the Camaro screeched off. I memorized the tag number, yelled to a nearby teacher to call the police, and it wasn't long before I heard sirens whooping like demented alley cats.

I bent over the boy, his warm blood soaking into my pant legs. His eyes stared blankly into the sun. Dead. I scrambled over him to Jimmy, who had taken a shot through the back. I later found out the bullet had passed very near his heart, but in that moment he was still alive, although blood kept spouting from his wound. With my help, he turned over, looked at me, recognized me, grabbed my shirt, and muttered a name, then another.

Two boys, who had been in one of Jimmy's classes, troublemakers both. Sons of former millworkers, I later learned from the police. The two hated authority. Hated school. Hated blacks. At times, so the story went, they occasionally fought with one another. Jimmy had had one of them expelled for fighting in his classroom. The other had later called Jimmy's apartment, screamed about the expulsion, and had threatened him. Of course, Jimmy had recognized his voice, and the next day he called the police and had the kid arrested. The gun I'd taken away, plus the tag number and the names Jimmy gave me, cinched it for the police. They corralled both boys at a local hangout within the hour and hauled them to the city jail.

Anyway, after giving me the names, Jimmy tugged at my shirt front.

"Remember Juanita?" he asked.

I nodded.

"Find her. Tell her I'm gone."

It was an odd plea, given that their two-plus years together had ended acrimoniously, but who was I to refuse a dying man his final request? So after I saw to it that Jimmy was buried – he didn't have a pot to piss in financially – and after I'd testified at the trial, the two boys glaring at me the whole time, I started looking for Juanita. I contacted the alumni association at U.T. Nothing. Then the Honduran embassy in Washington. Still nothing. She and I had had a big fight over her seeing Walt just before she moved in with Lucinda. And Luce and I, by the way, had never gotten anything going, because after Juanita moved in with her, Luce decided she didn't want me around. Anyway, I finally found Lucinda in Miami. She was busy, she said, promised to call back that night, although she didn't. Finally, months later, on a Saturday night, while I was grading papers, she called.

"You still interested in Juanita?" she asked rather peevishly. "God, Frankie, she was such a whore."

"A whore?" I asked, "What do you mean?"

She huffed. "The little twat kept running guys through our apartment as if we were operating a hooker palace. Same ones only a couple of times. It was like she was collecting penises before she had to go home and marry the creep her parents had picked out for her."

"Honestly, Luce," I said, "I know she could be passionate, but that doesn't sound like her."

"Well, you remember that Billy Joel song? 'You Catholic girls start much too late?' I don't know when she started giving it up, but she was clearly making up for lost time."

Her rant continued and that was beginning to depress me so I interrupted to explain that Jimmy, whom she'd never met but about whom she'd heard plenty from me, and, I'm sure, from Juanita, had been shot dead and he'd wanted Juanita to know about his demise. That quieted her, and she told me she'd kept tabs on Juanita, for reasons she didn't seem willing to explain, that Juanita had rebelled against her parents and the planned marriage, had refused to return to Honduras and had taken refuge in a Cuban émigré right there in Miami, an older man. They'd married and had had a couple of kids, both boys. She was now Juanita Duarte, not Armanda. That made it easy enough for me to track her down, so I called, got the voice mail, left a message, and more or less gave up on contacting her.

Then last night, a knock at my condo door.

The gray-haired lady gave me an all-too-familiar smile. She's broad in the hips now, but the mouth, the green eyes, they haven't changed. A smile, and then she said, in barely accented English, "Aren't you going to ask me in?"

Despite my shock at seeing this late middle-aged version of Juanita, I hugged her. To my surprise, she returned it, full-force. I stepped back to let her into my front room, and we sat, she on the couch, I in my recliner, the coffee table between us.

"I guess you got my message after all."

A nod. "And did I ever have a time explaining it to Hector, the world's most possessive husband. You'd think a seventy-six year-old man could let some things slide, but not Hector." She looked away. Her shoulders lifted and then sagged as she let out a slow sigh. "I hadn't been the most faithful of wives, but all that stopped after the birth of our two sons, and our relationship quieted down. At that point, Hector insisted that our import-export business was fine, just fine, without me helping him wine and dine his clients, so I stayed at home with the boys, and then after they were in school, I went back to college at the U. of Miami and got an Ed.D."

"A doctorate? In education?" I said, feeling unaccountably happy for her.

She eyed me, that same deep, ready-to-jump-me look from all those years ago, and then she nodded. "Hector had an accident not long after we married, and he ended up impotent. But that was okay, you know? It gave me latitude."

I tried to take in the implications of that, but I wasn't sure it made sense. Besides, what was she here for? Surely not another bed-squeaking love-a-thon. I found myself clenching the recliner's armrests, and to disguise my tenseness, I waggled my legs and leaned forward, trying to seem ready to take in her words more intently.

She eyed me, surely aware of my nervousness, but mature enough now not to take advantage of it. "Anyway," she said, drawing the three syllables out in true

Southern fashion, "after his accident, and with him knowing I was already sleeping around, we had an arrangement. I could breed – that's the way Hector put it later – with a couple of men that I selected."

"Really?" I interjected, "I'm surprised at that, what with the way I know Hispanic patriarchs are –"

Dual fires sparked in those green eyes. "No, Frankie, you don't know a thing about that. You don't. Yes, it's hard being a woman in our culture in a lot of ways, but in others it's comfortable, very comfortable. You just have to learn the rules of the game. And keep up appearances."

I glanced to the floor and said, "I was being patronizing, I guess. Sorry."

She bent to her purse, fumbled out a small folio, opened it to the first sheet, and handed it to me. "The first picture, that's our oldest, Hector Junior. Or I should say, he's the sixth. Flip it over. That photo is of Pablo."

My jaw gaped. Hector, the son, was tall, lanky, with longish, wavy black hair and a rather elongated face. He was dressed in what I can only call a sloppy fashion. I had the sense of a man who went about at home in baggy clothes, unshaven, hair untamed. Then Pablo: he was shorter, stocky, a full head of dark brown hair, and a prideful smile on his cherubic face. The two could have been clones of Jimmy and me at an earlier age. I handed back the folio without comment.

Juanita's rather enigmatic smile told me nothing. "I know it sounds terrible," she said, "but I had to go through a lot of young guys in order to figure out how to produce two sons with the physical characteristics of the only two men I had ever really loved. Two men who in a lot of ways were so much alike."

Nervous laughter burbled from me. "You loved us both? Really? I don't remember it that way."

She leaned forward, the smile turned to a harder expression, and she waved all that away. "You were both so insecure, but you were both so loveable. I needed you and Jimmy, and the two of you needed me, but in very different ways."

A thousand questions pummeled me, but I didn't know what – or how – to begin to ask.

"Oh, there were all sorts of risks involved in getting pregnant that way," she went on, "and there was never the guarantee that their genetics would trump mine." A smile. "But it was worth the risks. My sons are both good Catholic boys, and as I look at their pictures now, I know I have them to myself."

"Does Hector, the father, I mean, does he know what you've done? By re-creating Jimmy and me?"

She shook her head. "It wasn't any of his business. Not a part of our bargain."

"And the boys? Surely they must know something wasn't right about their coming into the world like that, you know, as some sort of genetics experiment."

Her eyes narrowed, but it failed to hide the tandem fire. She shook her head emphatically. "Despite my objections, they're daredevils, both of them. Windsurfing. Skydiving. Mountain climbing. Sports car racing." Her head hung, and she shook it, slowly, sadly. "But you know the paradox? In emotional things, I'm still their security blanket. The key is that their supposed father has always kept them at arm's length. No, if they knew the whys and wherefores of their births, they'd be really angry and I'd lose them. I can't have that, Frankie, I want them both with me until I die."

This struck me as a mother's fancy. "Surely they'll eventually settle down, marry, have children of their own. They won't always be there at your beck and call."

Again the fire in her eyes. "I taught children for years, but every school day during that time, all I could think about in my spare moments was my two boys, hoping they were all right, that when I got home they would still love me as much as I loved them."

For a few moments, silence hung between us.

"No," she said with adamantine finality, "they won't marry or have children. Oh, being vital boy-men they may get around some, but I'll never be apart now from the only two men I've been allowed to love without reservation. You can bank on it."

I wanted to ask questions, but my mind was so scrambled from these revelations that I couldn't. She sat there taking me in for another minute. Then she shut her purse, rose, kissed my forehead, strode to the door, and left, the way she'd done so many times before.

OBJECT OF AFFECTION

We're at the curb in her white BMW, preparing to brave late October's chilling rain. She's telling me, in the way she and I have come to converse, how you were born to greatness.

"I remember it as if it were yesterday," she says, her eyes a glistening red. "It was early morning and spring, and I was lying there trying not to relive the pain, a breeze straying through an open window of my hospital room. They brought Carlos to me, smiling in his sleep. 'He doesn't cry,' the nurses told me, 'he gurgles.' He had charmed one nurse to such a degree I was afraid she wouldn't let me have him. Eventually she did, and he nestled into my shoulder. A wonderful calm, I've always called it the calm of destiny, settled over us."

She reaches into her bag and lifts out a stitched-leather sphere. The once-supple covering has grown hard, a disease of cracks spread across its surface. "You see, it was always my dream. I wanted him to see the ball, to feel it, as soon as we got him home. I know he sensed something special about it when I placed it in the crib. He squirmed and turned to one side, and the ball bumped an arm, a hip. 'Don't be afraid,' I whispered to him. 'One day it'll make you great.' Then he looked up and smiled. He knew what the ball was going to mean to him."

"How?" I ask. "How could he have known? How could *you* have known?"

She fishes a tissue from her purse and blots a single tear. The rain has stopped and a high, humming wind is baring the sun, the poplars lining the street shaking free of their last leaves. "A child can sense his destiny, surely you would admit that."

"Yes, but I understand it's, well, unheard of in one so young."

A moment of happiness lifts her face. "But it's true. I could hear fame gurgling, see fortune in that beautiful smile. It was a mother and child thing, I suppose. Then Juan, that's his father, Juan lifted the ball and held it a foot above my baby's round face. Those big blue eyes searched until they found it. Juan leaned forward, barely able to hold the position because of the pain in that block-layer's back of his, and he lowered the ball, an inch or so from Carlos' nose. Carlos raised one chubby little hand and ran a finger down the stitching." She sighs. "He knew he was meant to play The Game."

The Game. She tells me that by six you were on the diamond, slapping the ball with authority, bouncing it from the child's tee through a maze of soprano crow calls along the red dust infield and onto the grass beyond.

Reaching for an inner balance, a counterweight for the void within, she continues. "From the start he was an athlete, a star, even. His talent, it just blossomed." She unfurls her hands to express it, imitating an opening flower. "But I wonder," she adds. Her gaze is traveling, chasing her thoughts, perhaps to a place even I have yet to visit, a place reachable only by the slow unwinding of mortal sorrow. "I wonder if he ever thought about it, you know? That the fans needed him to fill the holes in their own lives, to believe anything's possible." She watches a yellow leaf stumble across the windshield and drop to the glistening street.

"Sure," I say, "the athletes I've watched, they know the moments of greatness aren't just theirs. But do they appreciate the fans the way they should? Well, there are a lot of egos on the ball field." I realize she isn't listening; she's visiting some pleasure from your past.

"By the beginning of his senior year," she goes on, "every major college scout had a file on him, had visited him, courted him, made promises. He wasn't meant for college, though." She shakes her head, defiant. "It would have been a waste of precious years." Then she smiles. "So there we were, Juan and I, sitting in front of the television, barely breathing, watching his first major league at-bat. The count went to three and one before we heard him connect, and then the ball soared, cleared that green left field wall. The phone started ringing, just rang and rang. Juan took a couple of the reporters' calls and then he unplugged it. Later we watched Carlos run ten yards past the right field foul line and dive into the seats. He raised his glove, showed us the ball, and that ended the ninth inning."

She closes her eyes. "But you saw it, I think."

"I did. From above center field. I wasn't supposed to be there but, knowing what was to come, I had to see him for myself."

"He made the all-star team that year, and the next two years, too."

Then she gives her account of your fourth year, the year destiny's other shoe fell. Two hours before the season opener, you stumbled, fell down a flight of stairs at Yankee Stadium.

"It came on so quickly," she says. "He began dropping things, and not just in right field. He started slurring his words. The next year he was so embarrassed he quit giving interviews."

"You missed a few essentials, though," I tell her. "When you took over his press conferences, told the reporters how brave he was, how determined to beat the disease, I know you believed it. But he wasn't sure at all. He cried constantly, threw fits. Away from you, so as not to disappoint. But I saw them."

"I don't know about that," she almost shouts as she climbs from the car and bends into the wind. Then she stalks toward the chapel. Within, she strides without hesitation to the front, drops the ball into your casket. "It was a bad, a terrible year. I had my hands full with Juan's cancer."

Minutes later, a funeral staffer opens the chapel doors wide and others enter, heads down. Your mom slumps into a pew and her thoughts wander to your teammates as they enter, those burly, beer-swilling boy-men. One by one they take her hand, whisper words of comfort, hug her. She pats each one's broad, slumping shoulders, wipes tears from their bleary eyes, acknowledges with kisses the ones who are to bear your casket, whispers her appreciation for the way the team carried your waning athleticism that last season.

The service drones on, and a pair of your teammates comes forward. They reminisce, try to joke, then they break down. But even they know little of your helplessness after leaving the field, only the name: amyotrophic lateral sclerosis. They never witnessed the effort it took to perform the simplest tasks. They can hardly imagine the ordeal of fastening shirt buttons and tying shoelaces. It would have tested their mettle to see you struggle to chew your food and swallow, only to fall back exhausted, gasping for breath.

The priest invites the pallbearers forward for a last glance. Then other shoes begin whispering along the carpet.

I know, I should leave it at that, but I still can't get past your anger as your playing days ended. True, the fans expected too much, even after you began to stagger and fumble your words. But it was your mom alone, head now to her bodice, who rejected their cannibalizing expectations, the mom whose love you were sure you'd lost. The mom who took solace instead in shoring up your finances, so that toward the end she could surrender you to a hospice. Do you really think the outcome for you would have been different had she been there all day, every day, had it been she instead of the nurses keeping the television in your room tuned to games on ESPN? Had it been she instead of your social worker who sat with you for a half-hour each day, her hand on yours, the two of you watching recaps of the previous day's games? That it was this near-stranger who chose to be with you at the end, in the quiet hours before dawn? I doubt it. And the fans: for a while you were The Game to them, those fickle creatures. You knew that when your time in that legendary uniform ended you would die to them, so why the hurt, the anger?

Now your mother rises, and the others follow. When she reaches the casket she bends, turns, lifts the ball and holds it high. A jot of laughter breaks the solemnity, and your teammates applaud. She places the ball inside your right elbow, turns to scan the chapel's deeper reaches.

"He's here," she says, only to me.

"It's a common phenomenon," I tell her. "Maybe he doesn't yet understand the gulf he's about to cross. Or he's dredging for, you know, any crumb of love he might've thought he missed."

A man with delicate, white hands closes the casket and your mom surrenders to grief. One of your teammates guides her away. "Don't take him away," she moans into her handkerchief.

But she was right the first time – there you are in the back row, having again settled into that state from which it's possible to see me, for me to see you. I'm beside you in the span of a thought, and something within me gladdens as we exchange our version of a handshake.

"I thought it was you, the guy from the hospice who kept talking about crossing some river, right? Say, by any chance, do you know Gehrig?"

"He wanted to be here today," I say, dimming my effulgence, avoiding the deeper connection between us for one last tick of time, "but you know how it is with celebrity ex-athletes. There's always something, signings and such. He asked me to say hello." It's awkward, this unfinished role I have with you.

"Yeah, well, thanks for taking the time to stop by. Your play-by-play with Mom today has helped me work out a few things."

"I put it in a form you could digest, that's all," I reply, deflecting the gratitude, "and your mom does love you, despite what you think. It was never about money."

"Well, listen, man, I'm not mad anymore. We got this thing to do, right? So let's go."

That brightens me, brightens us both, and we slip outside, into the sun and wind. A gust takes us into the fog still hovering over the river. I point deeper into the mist and you nod. Whistling, head bent and hands in pockets, you disappear.

"*Vaya con dios.*" That's all I can come up with and, not knowing the language's nuances, I hope the phrase is consoling, hope it means I'll miss you, we all will, that The Game is transcendent and awaits you. Of course, I'll never know for sure. My fate remains that of a pilot, a steersman navigating others between two shores, and it will take me elsewhere, forever elsewhere.

But I do hear the rumors. They say your destiny in that place across the river will never have an off-season – your gifts are far too great for that. The fans there, they're already waiting for you, ordering beer, hot dogs, listening to The Game's raucous music as it swirls through an airy, ethereal stadium. There, they say, you'll forever find yourself suited up, knocking the dirt from your spikes, assuming your stance, taking the sign, then staring down the strike zone.

Myth has never been my cup of tea. But such stories are repeated so often I have to consider them larger than life. In them, you stride into the first pitch, a heater, low and a hair outside. Swinging with a rush of strength, you wreck the ball with that characteristic bark of wood on leather. You drop your bat, and the stadium hushes as the ball soars into darkness high above. You run at first, until you're sure, and then you grin and begin the trot, watching exhilaration tangible as the stadium's glare sweep over the field. The fans, they find that small, white speck as it emerges from the dark and follow its fall until it clatters into the centerfield bleachers.

It's at that point, they say, that something truly unique happens. If one watches carefully, one will note a faint, mist-like substance rise from the tiers of roaring fans and coalesce as a glow about the ball. It's a living symbol, the stories say, a sign that The Game, the fans, and you, are finally one.

COLLATERAL

DAMAGE

ONE

"John!"

I lean back and rub my eyes.

"John, are you up there?"

She knows I am, so I close out the word processing file I've been staring at and put my computer to sleep. Six steps and I'm to my grimy attic window. A stray Post-it has somehow attached itself to one of my house shoes. I peel it off and push the window up. Ozone-fresh air from the day's cold front invades the attic's musty smell.

She looks up, but she doesn't give me her usual smile and wave. She's so beautiful. The daily afternoon wind crossing Lake Lanier has overrun our thirty acres of pines and poplars and then moved on, giving her hardly a notice. Amazing. Coils of frizzy red hair bounce about her face. It's as if the ringlets are alive, as if they're about to fly, to soar with the hawks that keep calling from high above the lakeside cliffs. If I weren't so taken with her, I'd dash through the woods to the water's edge and climb up, to my favorite ledge, and watch the birds carve their majestic arcs in the sky.

She's standing beneath a dogwood, pawing at the grass with one foot, hips cocked to a provocative pose. Her arms, her face — they've lost their usual milky, dogwood-bloom hue. They're more the ruddy color the wind brings, the flush she says she hates and works so hard to cover up. She hugs her shoulders and turns sideways, trying to reduce exposure. So exquisite, even wearing the T-shirt, jeans, and sandals she changed into after work. Janet Fromme. Hard to believe such a beauty could be the managing editor of Gainesville's Times-Herald.

"John," she cries out, "I can't find him!"

Oh. The corners of her lips have turned down. The blue eyes that usually glisten with gaiety are now ominous slits. But maybe it's the growing shadows that have suddenly given her such an alien appearance.

I lick my lips, clear my throat. "Can't find whom?"

She punches dainty fists into her hips' curves and waggles her shoulders. Her voice rises, strained and hard. "Ted, John. It's Ted."

Now she's mad. Or maybe just scared. But whom did I think she meant? There are several possibilities. No, I'm not getting into that. Those names wouldn't mean anything to her. She'd ask questions, and my answers would cause yet more problems. "Ted," I reply. "Yeah. Ted."

Her chin trembles. A moan escapes her. Or it could have been the wind, I'm not sure. My thoughts are wandering, I need to pay attention.

"Please come help me, John," she begs. "It'll be dark soon."

It's hard for me to leave the attic; this is my safe place now, my home. The room's a dark space, really too gloomy for someone of my moods. An old gooseneck lamp attached to the top shelf of my desk hutch supplies most of its light. There's a week's worth of wadded papers thrown to the raw pine floor. And I need to shelve the open research books I've left scattered around the wallowed-out lounge chair I'm leaning across to consider Janet's plea. Cobwebs between and below the ceiling joists catch my eye, sinuous, diaphanous as so many ghosts. It's distracting to be this messy. Maybe that's why I haven't been able to write as much as a paragraph for days. Who knows? Maybe all I need is a little fresh air.

Ted. Ted's important, very important. Teen-aged boys need their fathers, and lately the waters between Ted and me haven't been particularly navigable. I wish I could reach him, to communicate with him on the deeper level of father and son. But Dr. Blucher tells me relationships between fathers and sons are always slippery.

All right, it's out the door and down the stairs. Come on, John, go. That's it. Somehow you missed the stairwell light. Just find the banister. The stairs creak, taunting me. I don't need this. Bad enough to be descending in such gloom. The dark's disorienting, making me dizzy. One hand finds the banister. I brace myself against the stairwell wall with the other. My thumb catches a splinter from the paneling. I reach the base of those twenty-one stairs without further incident and enter the foyer, pause a moment to rub my pulsing thumb before opening the front door.

No, I can't. It's so terrible outdoors at dusk — there're too many voices — a hell of nature's whispers. But I have to go. Ted. It's Ted. Janet can't find him. Please be there, Ted. For Dad. Okay, hit the downstairs light switches. Then one pull, and the door creaks open.

Strangely, it's not so bad this time — the wind has softened to a breeze. For once, its throaty whispers don't bother me. Cool grasses collapse across my house slippers, brush my ankles with a hint of dampness. A blue jay harangues from the roof's crown, then flies, its calls dissolved to nothing in the breeze's murmuring. I turn to peer through the trees and notice the sun sliding past Lake Lanier, its yellow slowly doused to a throbbing red.

Where's Janet? No. She can't be gone, too. Surely the woods wouldn't have taken them both. "Janet," I mumble. No answer. Can't see her. Too many things that shouldn't be here. Then, louder, "Janet!"

"Here," she calls, "by the big oak."

It's a wraith from the old cemetery on the next hill, not her. "Who are you?" My mouth's so dry the words clump in my throat. I have to cough them out.

"Damn it, John, it's me, Janet." Her voice softens, pleading again. "Please," she says, "we have to look for Ted."

It *is* her, it really is. I run, reach for her, my oafish momentum carrying me past and into the tree's rough bark. She sighs, motions for me to follow, and we turn toward the woods and the lake.

I stumble downhill behind her, through the underbrush. The dark, the cold, they're exhilarating now, even through my usual medicinal haze. Oh, this is nice.

This is the way a kid feels. No wonder Ted likes it here. Oh, yeah – Ted.

Janet stops and bends. "This is one of his smoking places." She glances up, probes my mind. "You didn't know he smokes?"

"No."

"Look around," she instructs, "there may be fresh footprints. Something, anything, to tell us he's been by here."

We're on hands and knees, peering through the drowsing light for depressions in the leaf mold, in the clay, still soft from rain. No footprints. No telltale signs. Nothing.

"There may be broken twigs or branches." Her voice grows in desperation. "Look quickly, please, John, before we lose the light."

No trail of broken vines or branches. No beer cans or cigarette butts. We edge down the path.

Ahead, a boulder looms, gigantic, the one guarding our path's end. She knows I don't like being this close to the water's edge at dusk, so she stays close, leads me around the monolith. My leading hand brushes past her trailing one. Teetering, I reach back, cram my fingers into a fissure in the boulder. The stone's cold, but at least I'm safe.

A new wind's risen here. It's pushing the water toward us in soft waves that laugh as they hurl themselves against the rocky shore. The hawks' cries flit toward me like skipping stones. Then the sun surrenders its last bloodstained light. Night slithers in. I'm blind to everything but the sky's last dim glow. I make out the first star, then another, then another.

Janet returns from a quick search of the shoreline, leans against the boulder, and stifles a sob. I reach out to cradle her face. My hand returns wet and strangely cold. Consolation, that's what she needs. It's my responsibility. It's terrible hearing her cry like this. But there's nothing I can do for her except hold her tight. She edges close. Careful, John – don't hug her too tightly. She's delicate, so delicate. She seems weightless, impalpable.

"What are we going to do?" she says into my shirt.

I have to comfort her. "Ted," I manage, "he's gone."

"Please, don't say that." Her crying begins again.

Can't think about Ted now, just want her to stop crying. Can't think. Wind. Voices. Their singing rises to laughter. Now they're inside my head. I can't make them stop. "What kind of writer are you?" they jeer. "Come on, John, say something – one simple, declarative sentence."

Janet turns toward the house. I follow. But this time the trail tilts sharply upward, taking us on a different path home. I scramble, almost crawling. Can't see the brush hanging over the trail until it scrapes my face. Rubble and wet clay give beneath my slippers and hands.

I have to follow the sound of her crying. My head feels like a balloon – totally devoid of anything helpful. Now, at least, the wind's taken her crying away. She's crashing through the underbrush somewhere ahead, but the noise is coming from all directions, chaotic, overwhelming.

A thud. She moans, swears. She's fallen. Then the wind's catcalls ease enough for me to hear her footsteps as she whispers through the trees and toward the house.

Or is it snakes I hear, hissing from the pine boughs? The poplar branches are heavy with them. See that big, diamond-shaped silhouette? That's one of them; that's its head. They laugh, too. "Come here, John," they're saying. "One little bite, I promise, then we'll leave you alone." Better run, catch up. Can't let the snakes see me like this, can't let them smell my fear.

Now Dr. Blucher's talking, somewhere inside me. "You have to ignore these things, John." It's the same thing he told me last week. "They aren't real."

"Then what is real?" I remember replying during last week's session. And how would you know what's real, I thought but didn't say, unless you've seen what I've seen?

He sat back, smiled, and reached into my thoughts. Mind control, that's his game. He wants to control me, to own me, the same way the wind and trees do. That's what he does, even when he interrupts my talking, which is most of the time. He muddies my thinking, plays games with my mind.

Now Janet's voice cuts through all this. Now the thoughts, the hisses, the odd things coming at me in the dark, they scatter like a flock of birds.

"John! Where are you?"

I've stopped. Somehow she's gotten behind me. "I don't know."

"Just walk slowly toward my voice," she calls out, firmly, gently. "One step at a time. Don't run. I know where you are. You're almost out of the woods. You're almost home."

If she only knew what's out here. All right, I'm doing it, for her. Maybe she's right. Maybe I'm almost out of the woods. But it's still a trek, a terrible, chilling, dangerous trek.

There's the porch light. The house is just ahead. She must've switched on the spotlight, because it's bright as noontime. Huh. Beyond the branches, is that the moon rising, so full, so reflective?

"Stop at the oak," she says, "catch your breath."

I stop for a quick gasp, but I'd be a fool to stay here long. Better count these long strides of mine, see how far away I am. Thirty-four of them, as I remember, from the edge of the woods to the porch.

There, I'm back. Up the porch steps, into the foyer light. I want to take her in my arms.

"Please, no," she says, slipping away to collapse into the rocker in our den. She bends to her upraised hands and begins to cry.

What am I supposed to do? We didn't find Ted. She keeps crying. Now I can't move. My mouth's dry and my eyes are burning. I'm rooted here in the foyer. All I can do is watch her cry.

She rubs her eyes dry, sighs, and reaches for the phone. She begins calling Ted's friends.

At last I can breathe. She's all right. I settle onto one end of the couch and flick on the TV. No reassurance there, so off it goes.

"No one's seen him all afternoon," she says a few minutes later, slipping onto the couch beside me.

I blow out a breath, the TV's square, gray eye returning my stare. My reflection – it's longer, gaunter than I remember – the elongated chin, the sagging, bony cheeks, the menacing bristles. Somehow, the furrows on my brow and cheeks have become ravines. When did this happen? Even those green eyes – they're piercing, and maybe a little savage-looking. The thick thatch of prematurely graying black hair points in all directions. Is that hulk of sagging bone and sinew and muscle wrapped in the rumpled red plaid shirt and baggy jeans really me, sitting beside Janet's tiny form?

Blucher tells me the sensation I'm feeling is called detachment. Some biochemical abnormality has caused it, probably the reason my writing has been so disengaged lately.

Janet leaps to her feet, so suddenly I can't help but jump. "I'm calling the county police," she says, her tone angry, determined.

She identifies herself. Someone at the station transfers her. She taps a foot, leather sandal slapping the oaken floor. She gives up a loud sigh, moves again to the rocker, and closes her eyes.

The standing lamp at the end of our ratty plaid couch is casting an oval light on the floorboards, just off the edge of the area rug. Uh, oh, something's wrong with the floor. An image of some sort is waving to me. Blink, John. It's still there, in the floorboards, beneath their dusty quilt, and now it's swirling. It slows, begins to shimmy, like a clump of cold Jell-O. Two beady eyes and a flat nose appear, and a mouth turned up at one corner in what may be a sneer. Sort of an irritated Kilroy. It was hiding there all this time, in the plane of our living room floor. Two brown, gnarled hands grasp the rug, and the thing lifts itself, like someone climbing from a swimming pool. It grows, standing now on two spindly legs, arms crossed above a distended belly. Fascinating, so fascinating. Who would have ever thought my life could be so full of such cheesy characters? But, strangely, their world is always inviting. So fluid, so creative.

No. Don't come any closer, please. It's not you I need, it's Janet.

Ted. Ted's gone – where is he? We're more than kin, he and I. We're brothers in the selfsame adventure, kicking and clawing for a way out. Ted thinks he's found an exit, I imagine. Fat chance. I tried running more than once. It didn't work. It just didn't.

Still waiting, Janet huffs, rises, and leans toward the kitchen, her back to me, jeans taut across her buttocks. She turns back. Those breasts. So exquisite. Maybe it's the fear, the danger she imagines for Ted, that makes her seem so vulnerable, so seductive. In the dim light, and despite the floor lamp's cone of red illumination, her skin tone has returned to dogwood white.

She gets so wrapped up in these things. But Ted's all right. I can feel it. I'm sure that's what this little fellow at the edge of the rug wants to tell me. You can tell by his posture, the way he stands there waiting for Janet's eventual loud, hysterical mini-drama with the police to end.

But I shouldn't care what this little fellow thinks. It – this person, creature, whatever – it's a figment of chemistry. That's what Dr. Blucher says. He's been insistent on my ignoring these guys. All right, I'll turn away, if that'll help. Easy, now. Don't make any false moves. These floor guys, you can never tell, they may go postal on you. No. It's no use. This thing, whatever it is, darts toward the window, grabs one of Janet's sheer white curtains and lets the outside breeze swing him. Now he hops to the sill, motions, points toward the lake. What's he saying? Oh. My name's Michael, he says. Now something about the cliffs. Well, I'm not going to listen. I shouldn't hear this sort of thing, not if I want to get well. Not if I want to stay alive.

No, it's Janet talking instead. She's yelling. Crying. She tells an officer at the police station that Ted's missing. Finally she calms down. "Yes, all right," she says with a long, moaning sigh. "They'll be here soon? Thank you." She smiles weakly. "Thank you. Thank you so much."

The call over, she wipes her eyes, glances my way, as if remembering something. She reaches into an end table drawer, shuffles through the mess inside. "Here, John. Take this." She opens an amber vial, tosses a capsule onto the couch cushions. I grabble for it as it slips into a crevice. Ah, there it is. Or is that the one I lost earlier this afternoon? It's so hard, keeping track of these things. But I'm not taking it. Not another medication. I'm afraid of them. "What is it?" I ask her.

"Just a mild tranquilizer. Dr. Blucher thought you'd need one from time to time." She smiles.

"I'll need water." When she gives me the water, I'll palm the capsule, then pocket it. Later I'll flush it.

Somehow she's managed to turn on all the downstairs lights, but when? That was another of Dr. Blucher's suggestions, lights would keep the hallucinations to a minimum.

Now she motions for me to follow her to the kitchen. I pick up the capsule and trail after her. She runs a glass of water half full from the tap and gives me a coy, challenging smile as she sets it on the kitchen table. "Go on, take it. And don't hide it under your tongue this time."

There's no way out. All right. I take it, wash it down.

We return to the couch. Still miffed at her insistence, I lean away from her, tap the maple armrest with a fingernail I've been chewing on. What's the big deal with this medication, anyway? It's doing nothing, absolutely nothing.

Well. I can't think of anything to say, and Janet's quiet, too. The grandfather clock in the dining room makes soft, relentless tocks as it chases time. After a few minutes, my muscles release. The medication, it must be working. Tension leaves me as if from a faucet turned on full blast. Okay. My thoughts are clearer, less threatening.

Gee, this is normal. I can't help chuckling. Not bad, I guess. But normal's not for me, not anymore.

A hard rap on the front door. Our silence has been so thick, so calming. An intruder. Maybe I should call Dr. Blucher. I can't look. Janet rises and answers.

"Ma'am," a uniformed county cop says, a burly one with stout shoulders and bandy legs, "you called that your son's missing?"

"Ted, yes." She stands aside, an arm outstretched in my direction.

The cop and his partner nod, step inside, and blink as they adjust to the den lights.

"We've looked everywhere," she continues. "We've called friends, anyone who might have seen…" Her voice breaks, the sentence vanquished by a held-back sob.

The second uniform steps up. He's taller and leaner than the first. "May we have a seat?"

Janet sighs. "Of course."

They pick their way across our den's clutter, taking in everything in sight as they move. They're eying me, too, and Janet notices. Palm up, she flicks her fingers, a silent command for me to stand and shake hands.

Well, I'm not going to. Dr. Blucher, he should know about this. He never said the hallucinations would be this real.

Janet's shoulders slump. She gives me a fleeting, resigned grimace. "This is John, my husband."

Oh, what the hell. Dr. Blucher says it's all right to go along with these figments as long as I remember they aren't real and don't get too wrapped up in them. I start to my feet, but the first cop smiles and waves me back. They stand as if waiting for a more precise invitation to sit. Janet directs one to the rocking chair, the other to a straight-backed cane-seat chair opposite the couch.

"We'll need a description," the first cop announces. He wriggles the rocking chair back a fraction of an inch.

"I have a school picture," Janet says. "Will that do?" She rummages in the end table drawer as I stare at the carpet.

I'm tense again. More medicine, she's going to give me more medicine. No, that's not it. She smiles and slips back next to me, her blue eyes glistening. She leans toward me. It's a tiny color photo. Ted. His swirls of flaming red hair and pale, almost translucent skin are Janet's, the jutting chin, and long, angular face mine. The freckles were Ted's own contribution, I suppose. In this photo he's unsmiling, even hostile.

I don't know why he won't smile. He's such a friendly kid – or was. It's been maybe three years since he was up emotionally. These past two years, he's been different, so different. Janet writes it off to teen angst, but I don't know. I just don't know.

"His height?" the second cop asks. He takes Ted's photo and pushes it under the metal hinge on his clipboard. "We need that, his approximate weight, what clothes he was wearing when last seen."

Janet gives him that information and tells him to keep the picture. She jumps to her feet and scurries into the kitchen.

The first cop keeps staring at me, evaluating. Now he turns to Janet, who has returned with two mugs of coffee, the aroma somehow eluding me. "Is Ted a happy kid?" the cop asks. "Has there been any trouble at school? Any evidence of drug use?"

"No," she replies, as she hands off the mugs. "He's good, well mannered. His schoolwork has always been fine. In fact, he's still on the honor roll, although his grades have been slipping a bit, especially science and math. And he never forgets his chores." She glances at me, nervously, as if she wishes I weren't here. Then she adds, "But lately Ted's been a little uncommunicative." She collapses onto the couch. Her head touches my shoulder, so softly. Then she straightens.

I consider putting my arms around her, but I don't. She doesn't seem to mind my lack of response, though. And, anyway, I have things on my mind. Like why doesn't she mention Ted's cigarettes and beer. Where does he get those things? But maybe they're not that important; otherwise the cops would've asked about them. Janet says it's only experimentation, so it can't be a big deal.

The cop who's been eying me sips his coffee. I try to look away. He clears his throat. That intense look, it reminds me of Dr. Blucher. I can't get away from this man. I'm his mental prisoner.

"Mr. Fromme," he asks, "do you have anything to add here?"

My mouth is dry, so dry. My hands begin their familiar nervous dance. The medication's already wearing off. "Ted," I tell him, "he's gone."

The two cops sit upright. They're staring through slits now.

The first policeman asks, "Sir, what do you mean by that?"

Janet stands, moves between the cops and me. "John is fine, just fine." After a pause, she adds in a less firm tone, "He has a disorder, that's all."

The first cop looks perplexed until the other one turns to him and whispers, "Nuts."

This time Janet's voice shrills. "He has schizophrenia, all right? Most of the time he's fine. He takes medicine for it, and he works regularly. He's a novelist, a freelance journalist. Do you know how much mental effort that takes?"

"We're sorry, ma'am," the second one says, without a hint of contrition. "We have to ask. Is he dangerous? Could he have done something with Ted?"

"No!" she screeches. "Schizophrenia doesn't make a person dangerous." She swallows. "At least not very often. And don't talk about him as if he weren't in the room. Don't you think he has feelings?"

They rise, heads bowed, the first one saying they'll be back in the morning to look through the woods. They'll also put out a bulletin, check a few places before they come.

"No!" Janet howls. "Check now, before it's too late."

She's coming unhinged, crying again. I reach for her. One goofball in the family is enough. She swats at my extended arms, but misses.

The second cop starts to protest, but the other waves him quiet, saying, "All right, ma'am, we'll see what we can do." They're taking turns talking to Janet in low, apologetic voices, their tone full of concern. She glances my way and sighs. Their voices soften to consolation. The two exit, clomp across the porch, down the steps, and begin to comb our woods, yelling back and forth and shining lights with long, powerful beams.

It's late; I've forgotten to take my next anti-psychotic. I fumble a pill case from my pocket. Janet tells me to get off the couch, go to the kitchen, get some more water. All right. I go, swallow the pill and a mouthful from the glass I left on the kitchen counter. Soon everything will be on an even keel again.

An hour later, the cops give up. No sign of Ted. Janet offers them more coffee. They accept, ask more questions about his habits, his friends, places he might haunt. I feel the need to join in this time, to show them I'm okay, that I can handle situations.

"Ted," I tell them during a lull in the questions, "I don't think he likes me. Not like he used to."

"How's that?" the first one asks.

Janet's beside me on the couch again, and she holds up a hand. "Are you sure you want to get into this right now, John?"

My smile must be reassuring, because she leans close and returns the smile.

"Ted used to be so happy," I tell them. "He was always joking. He laughed at everyone else's jokes. Used to pull pranks. Funny things."

"For instance," the first one prompts.

"Tell them about the laundry episode," says Janet. She's smiling, too, a genuine one for the first time this evening. Her gaze falls to the rug, into the past, where the fun used to be, for all three of us.

"Wednesday nights were dance nights," she says. Her relating this makes me chuckle. She laughs into my shoulder. Her hand passes so close to mine that I can feel her warmth. Then she turns to the policemen.

"We'd roll up the rug," she begins. She jabs a finger at our stained Belgian version of a Persian area rug.

I'm really feeling settled now, so I nod and pick up the story. "Ted, his Wednesday afternoon chore was to do the laundry. That particular night, it was eight p.m., and he hadn't started yet."

"We both work long hours," Janet explains. "Ted was eleven then, and his doing the laundry helped a lot."

"I imagine he bucked the traces when you suggested it," the second cop remarks, shifting in his chair. "I know my kids would."

Janet shakes her head vehemently. "He suggested doing it. He was that way."

"He was that way," I chime in.

"Go on, then," the first one says.

I'm lost in a fog of memory. Maybe I'm telling this to them, but I'm not sure. Ted wanted to dance with us, but we told him he had responsibilities.

"Doing the clothes is your job, remember?" Janet said. "Get that done, then we can all dance together."

So he plodded off to the laundry room.

We had an old console stereo back then, over by the west window, a hand-me-down in a scarred maple cabinet, from Janet's parents, and a stack of their records. The Mamas and the Papas. Tommy James and the Shondells. Herman's Hermits. Paul Revere and the Raiders. The Young Rascals. And, of course, the Beatles. We always saved *Meet the Beatles* for last, mostly because that was Ted's favorite, and a great way to end the night. That amazing band at its best, before rock 'n' roll succumbed to pretense. So we started out with the Mamas and the Papas – "California Dreamin'" and those songs. The male voices were so pure, so chilling in their modal melodies, the ladies' soaring harmonies bouncing along on top. Talk about perfection.

I would unscrew the end table lamb bulb and the one for the floor lamp, replace them with blue and red ones, and set out an old lava lamp. A few seconds later, eerie shapes would begin congregating on the pine paneling and open oak rafters. The room took on the feel of a 'sixties/retro nightclub.

That night Janet cranked up the stereo a bit. The record crackled for a second, then the next song swelled, sounding through the rafters and tumbling down the pine paneling. The windows began to rattle. The curtains, now turned red and blue, shimmered. We kicked off our shoes, started the free-form dance stuff we learned from Janet's parents. Before long, and despite the November cold that had invaded the house, we were sweating. But the music thrilled us, lifting us to a dance we hadn't learned and weren't making up. It was as if we were watching ourselves dance, the music moving our bodies in ways only the music knew. Denny and John's voices, shored by Michelle and Cass' delicate, lyrical countermelodies, engulfed us.

The tasteful backbeat and subdued flute parts on those cuts gave full flesh to the vocals, the rhythms somehow sneaking in to sweep us up, carry us away. Beautiful. Just beautiful.

Then another album, some group I can't now remember. After that, Janet put on a single, "Dedicated to the One I Love." Our song. We close-danced, her T-shirt damp, the nape of her neck rich with that morning's touch of Chanel.

Wow, I think to myself, I'm getting aroused just thinking about it. God, I want her. After all these years, I still want her so badly.

Anyway, we kept dancing our way through the record stack, then took a beer break. No sign of Ted. We could hear the washer chugging. On the rare occasions when he was late doing the wash and we were dancing, he'd at least peek around the corner, offer a few clumsy, pitter-patter dance steps. But not that night. We didn't hear a peep from him. Janet gave me that concerned look she always wore when Ted was out of her sight for long.

Finally we heard maybe a dozen clumsy steps, as if he was stumbling. A long silence, followed by the pounding of sock feet on the hall floor. Janet laughed and pointed. Ted was peeping around the corner.

She sighed her relief, hands molded to her hips. "Come on out," she called. "You can dance until the dryer stops. Then we'll help you fold things and put them away."

"You sure?" he asked, eyebrows bobbing, hands gripping the door casing.

"Come on," I assured him, and waved him into the den.

"You sure?" he asked again, a low giggle escaping him.

Janet's brow wrinkled, and then she laughed. "Ted, just what are you up to?"

He pulled himself around the corner and into the red and blue light. He had put on a complete load of wet clothes — Janet's, his, and mine. Jeans and shirts first, underwear on top. His final touch was a pair of Janet's black lace panties. He held an old Atlanta Braves cap, and this he tugged over his ears at a rakish angle. Wiggling his butt, as much as he could with all those clothes on, he sprayed a fine mist into the air.

"I'm ready to par-tay!" he squeaked in his pubescent voice, and gave us his best John Travolta *Saturday Night Fever* imitation. Water puddled about him.

"You're wet," said Janet, hand to mouth, not sure whether she should laugh.

"All wet," I agreed, "totally wet."

"Totally radical," Ted corrected. "I'm wild and crazy." Little did he know then about wild and crazy.

Janet put on *Meet the Beatles*, and Ted began to whirl, like a deranged dervish.

"Spin cycle," Ted yelled.

Janet wiped away sweat and approached close enough to be swatted by his mist.

Then a thunk. His feet slid through the puddle. He landed on his back, his arms and legs flailing like an upturned turtle.

"Let this be a lesson," I said. "Never do wash on the den floor."

"Pretty crazy," the first cop says. He blanches, aware of his poor choice of idioms. "Was he always that way?"

"Only on Wednesday nights," I reply.

Janet eyes the pair and sighs. "It was fun. A way for us to blow off a little harmless steam."

"Well," the second cop comments, "we're not experts on normal, but that kind of stunt seems a little bit out there."

"All right," the first one says, slapping his knees, clearly a move to keep the other from further elucidation on the out there comment. They rise in unison, like marionettes, as if the move had been orchestrated.

"We'll let you know if we hear anything," the first one says. "And if Ted shows up, be sure to call it in." He gives us his card.

Janet sees them to the door. She stands just inside, watching as they again clomp down the porch steps, then bang the car doors shut and edge down our gravel drive toward the road to Buford. She lifts her gaze to mine, her expression that of a frightened little girl. I want to kiss her, but I can't. My head's buzzing. The voices are returning. I think Janet wants sex, consoling sex, the first time in three months, and now this. I can't, not with this buzzing going on – who knows? certainly not me – but it might be contagious.

Before I can put a stop to things, we tumble onto the couch, the beginnings of a make out. She must want Ted off her mind. There's nothing I want more than to respond deeply, but I can't, not with this buzzing. And maybe Ted's on my mind, too. Sure. Of course he is. He's my son.

My eyes are closed, but I think she's wriggling a hand into my jeans. Nothing. Wet noodle city. Once again, my body's not my own, something taking it over. An unfamiliar voice: Ezra, that's his name, he says. I stiffen, but not like that. I can hardly breathe, I'm so tense.

Janet knows. She always knows. "Just relax, baby," she purrs. Her tongue almost grazes my face. Now what? In my ear? Ordinarily that would be enough to turn on the Pope, but not me, not now.

She stops and edges away. I open my eyes and notice she's staring, the way the cop did. She's trying to control my thoughts, too, make me do what she wants. But that won't work tonight. The others, the voices, Michael and Ezra and all the others, they're too interfering for that. She moves toward me, wants to kiss me, but I'm immobilized. I can't even pucker. Nothing.

Once again she slides away, against the armrest. She's hurt. I can tell by the way her mouth is scrunched up. Why can't I ever do anything right?

"I'm going to bed, John. You do whatever you want."

She stomps up the stairs, and the bedroom door slams. I'm alone again, except for Ezra's hoarse voice.

"See that, John?" he says. "We made her go away. Now we can play. What do you want to do?" But I don't want that tonight. Ted. I have to figure this out. Where can he be?

Something flits past at the periphery of my right eye. It's Lana. "Don't worry about her, John," she says. "You should relax, baby. You know I'm available, if that's what you want. Wow! Do you know how hot you are?" She cocks a hip.

Ezra laughs. He's talking to Michael. "She doesn't care about him," says Ezra. "She just wants to do him. Drain him. Leave him limp and sticky. Starch the sheets."

"I don't know," Michael says. "Maybe he shouldn't get involved at all. A breath of fresh air, that's what he needs. Sit on the cliffs with his feet in the water, touch a few stars, sing a few songs. There's a meteor shower tonight. The Piscids, I think. Or maybe it's the homonyms. No, he needs a pause for the cause."

"Not the Piscids." Ezra again. "That'll remind him of sex. All that stuff shooting this way and that."

Michael laughs. "Raise the drawbridge," he yells. "I'm coming through!"

"Coming," Ezra agrees. "Becoming, maybe. No, that's Ted." He turns and winks. "Right, John?"

I can't stand any more of this. Falling back, I cram a pair of throw cushions against my ears and start humming. I imagine looking at the stars, my feet in the lake. Good, that drowns them out, at least for now.

A deep breath and a glance around. Oh. I'm inside the house. Its timbers start to groan as the temperature drops, the grandfather clock tsk, tsk, tsking. Who asked his opinion, anyway?

Three hours go by, maybe four. All the lights are off but the standing lamp. The clock chimes five times, so I'm sure I've slept some. I realize I need Janet, really need her, the way she wanted. But she's asleep now. Maybe I can just lie beside her, feel her softness. But she's angry when I do that. Can't blame her, can I?

Light from the open attic window, through the upper door I left ajar, is allowing shadows to infiltrate. They're as alive as the full moon. Maybe the voices belong to these shadows. Turn on a light. No, can't risk that. Just climb the stairs, John. The voices, the shadows, they won't bother you if you ignore them. That's what Dr. Blucher says.

The landing creaks a little under my weight, then I'm at the bedroom door. Janet usually locks it from the inside when she's miffed. No, it's open. She wanted me to come in. She planned it this way.

The brass knob is cold on my hand. The door whispers open. She's raised the window, for fresh air. That's the way she sleeps best, with a breeze stirring those gauzy white curtains. They're dancing. Monday, Monday. They heard me thinking about dancing with Janet and Ted. They're so delicate, so graceful.

The moon's halfway up. Its light spreads, reaches through the open window to Janet, and caresses her face. So beautiful. I want her so much. But I can't – she'll be angry. The last time I tried that, she was really, really upset.

Gently, very gently, I lift the padded bench from her vanity, set it near her. Good. I can watch over her, the way she's always watching over me. So beautiful. She's sleeping naked. She still wants to. No, John, you can't do that. She has to wake up first.

In the bathroom I try to pee, but I can't. Anyway, all I'd accomplish is spraying everything within reach. Just stand. Relax, it'll come. I was right; I spray the wall, the floor, the toilet. The hand towel, wipe up everything.

Back on the bench. She's still asleep, beginning to snore into her pillow. So beautiful. I can't stand it, so I fumble with my zipper. I grow and grow and grow and grow and grow. Stroke. It's the only way. Stroke. Stroke. Strokestrokestroke. Oh, into the towel, yes, into the towel, not into her this time. Into the towel. She's so tiny and fragile. Oh, God. Oh.

TWO

Morning light has long since found the attic. It's cold, especially at this hour, and it's a little dank. Lana has spooned into me on the cot. Sensing I'm awake, she whimpers and snuggles deeper. But there's no warmth to her, no softness, no feel of femininity. As the low hum in my head begins, she sighs, turns, works herself onto one elbow and smiles knowingly. It's as if she senses my unease, the pre-composition jitters I always feel at this time of day. I expect another of her erotic come-ons. Instead, she turns wistful, her gaze on something far away. "The other writers I've been with," she says, "they're all suffering some form of impotence. Some of it's physical, some emotional, but a lot of it's simply mental – writer's block, you know? All in the cause of art, they keep telling me. But I think it's really a case of trying too hard to squeeze art from their sex drive."

Her voice has become so clear, so intimate, much more so than Janet's. I'm rapt now as she clambers up to look me in the face.

"What I want to know, though," she goes on, giving me a leer and a wink, "is why can't all writers be as full in the flesh as you? Render unto Caesar what is Caesar's, I always say, but give your body to me." Her come-hither look slides into a fetching, little girl gaze. She giggles.

I have to look away. My God, I think, who are you? What are you? If she's a figment, what's this telling me?

Another giggle, and this time her voice is coming from everywhere, from nowhere, maybe from my own thoughts. "If I'd known you were this good in bed, I'd have come when you were younger, when we both were younger." She sniffs. "Before you hooked up with that awful woman."

My first impulse is to protest, to tell her Janet's sensitive and caring and attentive. But what's the use? It'd be like talking to the wall.

I push away, feet to the floor, and slump, head in hands. Lana tumbles softly to the floor. Every night and morning it's like this. At night I have to pull this uncomfortable cot from my tiny attic closet, open it, and set it here, before the lounge chair by the window. Sleeping this way's not easy, especially on full moon nights. But to get my best work done I have to get up early, at dawn if possible, before Janet and Ted rise for work and school.

Solitude, that's my device, that's how inspiration comes, with no interruptions, no extraneous influences. For me, writing's become a gestalt, a process to define what's going on in my mind. It allows me to give voice to so many people, so many situations, simultaneously. After all, isn't that what this age is about? Social and personal fragmentation, struggling to find some deeper sense of identity?

Lana's still whispering, bawdy things she's sure will arouse me. Finally, she sits on her heels, chest pushed forward, eying me to gauge the effect. "It's incredible how horny you were last night," she remarks. Her expression is determined now. Then she sighs and rolls onto one side, caresses a naked, inviting hip with the palm of her free hand. The movement starts her breasts rolling, almost liberating them from that red negligee.

Why does she insist on provoking me like this?

Her voice slips into my thoughts. "It's what I do, John. It's, like, you know, a job. But last night was a real turn-on for me. I want you to know that. It's never been that way with the others. You're the best, the absolute –"

"Stop it!" I'm beyond interest in this; I just want to get to work. My neck hurts from sleeping without a pillow. I rub it, but it doesn't ease the cramping. I have to get the *Atlantic* article done, but first I need to get rid of bigmouth. Bigmouth. Huh. A joke there, you know?

"Oh, come here, John," she taunts, beckoning, her hand and arm miming a snake's movements. "You know how to make me shut up, I know you do. Remember? The way you did last night. You gagged me good. I still can't believe it. You're really something, did you know that?"

Standing, I glare. Then I stretch and scratch.

"All right," she says with a sigh. She rolls away, offering me a view of that shapely derrière. A waggle, then a look back, checking for response.

I give her nothing.

She sighs again, rises. Hips like ripe, sexy pendulums, she glides silently into a corner morning hasn't yet negotiated. She disappears.

It's been this way for the past two years. All that trash talk of hers, getting me aroused, then nothing. No wonder I have problems making love to Janet. How am I supposed to know whether these come-ons of Lana's are real? How do I know which woman is the real deal?

Come on, John. You know it's Janet. Her touch is warm. She cries and smiles and loves and gets angry.

Despite Lana's trashy, voluptuous unpredictability, there's a sameness to her. I don't know what it is, exactly. She's more than willing to act out any and everything I imagine, as if she were the omega of my deepest desires. But somehow, she's as rote as a robo-call, as if her provocations are a script she's memorized and repeats to the point of nausea. At least that's the impression I'm left with. Most of the time I don't remember much of what she does. Really, I don't. The buzzing starts, then she's there, talking that way, arousing me, and the next thing I know it's over, and I end up with absolutely no sense of satisfaction. Maybe it's the medicine. There are always side effects. Yeah. That has to be it. Medications don't cure anything, they treat symptoms.

Now the whole thing – Lana and Janet and my writing – has me antsy. I have to pace. Wave your arms, John. If that doesn't make the buzzing stop, there's always yelling. Janet doesn't like that, though, and I don't blame her. It makes me sound crazy. Yahhh! Flap, flap, go the arms, like a goony bird. Loony bird. Damn it, get to work!

A glimpse at my blank computer screen as I stumble by, and I freeze, some elfin figure reflected there. It's Vince, isn't it? Stop, John. Look closer. Oh. It's me, reduced to a six-inch figure. Please, don't let it turn into Vince. I have work to do. Quick, look around!

Ah. In the attic window's grimy panes. There I am. The real me – hair matted, jeans and flannel shirt wrinkled and twisted. You need a shave, John. You're a wild man, where once there was a clean-cut, handsome, successful writer. "All right," I sigh aloud, "I get it. Take a bath. Shave."

The stairwell from the attic looms, still dark, the stairs steep. Eleven of them, not enough to cause the kind of claustrophobia I get from the ones to the ground floor. One step at a time, John. One, two, three…

That's better. The bathroom light's on. The hanging plants of Janet's, the philodendron and fern, they move imperceptibly, still green, but wilted, definitely in need of watering. Why doesn't she do that anymore? No shower for me, though, all that water hissing like snakes, laughing at me. A tub bath. At least that way I can get in after the hissing stops. The faucet sputters, then coughs, and the tub begins to flood.

Steam's rising, wispy fibers of it. It's okay, they're disappearing into the hanging greenery. Look, past the sweaty, slate gray walls. Drops are forming on the stippled ceiling. They're watching, like dozens of faraway eyes. Don't let them do that, John, look away and slide into the tub, inch by inch.

Ah, that feels good. I'm sweating already.

"That's the way I like it," says Lana from the periphery of my vision. "I like my men hot and sweaty." She vamps her way into full view from the bathroom door, still in the red negligee. She bends over the tub to afford me another look at those breasts. "You want me to jump in with my clothes on? That's one of your fantasies. You told me so last night, don't you remember?" She eyes me, mischievously.

I can't let those eyes of hers get to me. They're a deep, bottomless blue, like the lake. Something in them wants me, all of me. She wants to dominate. Look away, close your eyes, John. But she's moved even closer. I can sense it.

"Oh, come on, admit it," she whispers, as if her lips were at my ear, "this is a turn-on for you. Let me get my negligee and panties wet. It'll seem as though I'm naked, but you won't be able to see a thing. All you'll get is a suggestion of what's underneath, and that'll drive you wild. After that, you can peel them off me. Like a slow tango."

This is starting to bother me, really bother me. I don't remember a thing about a tango. "Go away!"

"John," she scolds, smirking.

"You don't really exist. That's it, isn't it, Lana? You're not real. Dr. Blucher says so. He says you're a figment."

She laughs, eyes me, my groin suddenly groaning, throbbing. "If I'm not real, then what's that?" She points to my erection.

"I don't know. Go, get away!"

She pays no heed, climbs in, immerses herself. Her clothes are sopping, clinging. She wriggles out of the panties, settles onto me.

But I don't feel a thing. Not a damned thing. She's so available, yet so unavailable. The opposite of Janet.

Janet won't have anything to do with me, for the most part. All right, my clothes get smelly, I can understand her not liking that. But it gets stuffy in the attic, especially in summer. Do you have any idea how much energy it takes to bathe? It's hard enough to undress. Then there's the soap, the shampoo, rinsing off, and toweling dry. It's so draining.

I don't sleep well, that's what makes waking up and living this routine such a chore. Get up tired, stay tired. All this mental work, just to make a living. Need to save my energy for writing. You're an adult, John. You have a family to support. No, don't start that. It brings back memories, bad ones, Mom haranguing Pop all the time. All the time.

"Relax, baby," Lana soothes. "I'll do all the work." She begins her up-and-down.

Water should be slapping the tub's sides; she should be making waves, water slopping onto the floor. Why isn't the water cascading? Why isn't it being fooled? Am I easier to fool than water?

Actually, she and Janet are both figments, each in her own way. Janet, withdrawn now, most of the time withholding, Lana incapable of anything but talk. So how do I choose? Janet or Lana, which way? Maybe I can get away, make them both leave me alone, work something out.

But what is it I'm supposed to work out? And how? If I could just get some sleep, wake up refreshed, the way I used to. Tired, sleepy. This water's so relaxing.

Coffee, that's what I need, but Janet won't let me have it. She's my guardian. She's keeping the Huns at bay until I can manage to work something out. Guardian? Huns at bay? That's a laugh. Get up, John, quit the wishful thinking. Dry off, find some clean clothes and get to work.

"Ooh," says Lana. "You're the best, John." She settles into the other end of the tub, her legs across mine. Another faraway look. "I've had so many men, you know? Each one's been so large and virile, like you. But none of them, not a one, has been as good as you. I don't know, you give me tingles, inside and out. I've never had that before."

Good for her. As for me, I'm numb, can't feel a thing, anything important, that is. But these odd urges, the strange, itchy sensations, I wish they'd go away. They keep me twisting, turning, keep me up, awake, all night long. No energy to write. But I have a deadline, an article. Come on, get up.

The bathroom's cold. Towel off quickly. Get dressed. Uh. My jeans are as grimy as the attic window. I can feel the grit and oil in the material. Ugh. Shirt's smelly, too.

Janet hid my clean clothes. Why does she do that? Does she want me to go around naked? One of these days I'll have a weak moment and people will see what's going on inside me. What will she do then?

These dirty rags will have to do, I guess. Comfortable, actually. Oh, man, this shirt stinks. Maybe I should wash clothes. No, that's Ted's job. Save everything for him.

Ted. Janet screamed his name last night. A dream woke her. She saw me. She saw what I was doing. She pushed herself to the bed's far side, to a prayerful, kneeling position, her exposed skin aglow in the moonlight. So tempting. White as milk. Beautiful.

She screamed again, at me, I think it was. Yeah, I'm sure she meant it for me.

"No! Don't do that!" she said. Then the yelling turned to moans. "Stop it, John, please!"

I finished then, wiped myself. My smile must have seemed more apologetic than reassuring, because she started bawling, really bawling. Circling the bed and attempting to hug her didn't help. She edged away and screamed again. Then she gasped, fell to the bed and drew the sheet about her, one breast still winking. So beautiful. The sobs she couldn't keep in turned to hysterical moans. She buried her head in a pillow.

"Sorry," I explained. But that's crazy. What did I do, something so awful? Nothing more than she does for me sometimes. "I just wanted you, the way we were going to, last night, downstairs."

"Just stop it!" she raised her head, eyes glistening with anger. Then anguish poured down her cheeks in rivulets, stray tears twinkling like stars.

She batted at her wet cheeks and glared. This was something new – a glare so intense it could have killed. A glare like mine; I've seen it in the bathroom mirror. She stumbled to her feet, clicked on the light, grabbed clean underwear and a dress and stalked toward the bathroom, dragging the sheet. She eyed me furtively, as if I were some sort of freak she had to escape.

Water began to run. I froze, just outside the bathroom door. She's in there, with the hissing. Is she all right?

After a while, the hissing turned to soft grunts and thumps. She must be toweling. Little noises, tiny, delicate ones, as she dressed. The door opened.

Groaning at the sight of me, she stamped, threw her towel, just missing me. "Just leave me alone, John! Please!"

She started crying, and I almost did, too. She stepped toward me, still a little sweaty from the shower. Probably realizing I still wanted her, she backed away.

"I have to be at the paper in a half-hour," she said, firmly and with finality. "It's strategic planning. I'm making a presentation. We have decisions to make before work hours. I can't be late for this."

"You have to go? At this hour?"

"Yes, John, at this hour."

Who was she trying to fool? Desire — I could tell she was holding back desire. She didn't have a meeting; that was a lie. She wanted to make love. I could see the sparks in her eyes as I walked her back to the bedroom, but she was afraid to admit to it. I know, I should have left her alone. Instead I reached for her.

She ducked, eluding me. I lost my balance, somehow jammed my hand between the bed frame and the mattress and springs.

"Ow!" A spring's rough end had gouged deep enough to set a tiny drop of blood free. I rubbed the spot.

"Why'd you do that?" I moaned. "I was only trying to love you."

She strode past, eyed me cautiously as she put on a mastodon bone necklace. She ran a hand through her matted hair, each tug leaving her red tresses fuller. The curls grew until her hair was a thick, coiled mass hanging to her shoulders. So appealing.

"Please eat something this morning." Her words were both cold and tender. "I'll leave out some bagels. Take your medication. That's very important, John, you have to take your medication. And try and find Ted, will you?"

A blink. I swallowed, hard. "How?"

"I don't know!" She tensed, as if contracting her muscles would help her secure some lost emotional handle. "Call those policemen. Look in the woods. Ted may be hiding from us. He may have taken his sleeping bag, so he could be alone. I don't know, just do something!"

"The – my deadline," I stammered.

"He's your son, John, you have to do something." She turned, and with a partly stifled wail, she fled down the stairs and into the kitchen.

A peevish clattering rose from there. It grew louder. Coffee aroma wafted up the stairs. The scent of it grounded me a little. The front door slammed, and then the door to her SUV. The car's tires growled in pneumatic protest as they crunched down the gravel drive.

Then not a sound, except for a faraway barn owl. So I trudged up to the attic and to my cot.

Now it's late morning and I'm way behind schedule. And I'm hungry. I work my way down the steps again. One. Two. Three...

"Hey, John," says Lana, "I'm still here."

She's standing in the bathroom doorway, naked and dripping water, her back against the jamb, knee cocked in an Irma La Douce pose.

"We can do it all day," she whispers hoarsely, her tongue flicking to catch the drops of sweat and bath water slipping down her cheeks. "When the sun starts falling, we can run naked through the woods, to the lake, up the cliffs. We can do it there, too, if you want. And when we're finished we can roll onto our backs and feel those last warm rays on our bodies." Then, quicker than the eye can follow, she's on me, as much as that's possible, embracing, pressing, tugging.

A tingle surges up and down my spine. I run, down the stairs and into the kitchen, rub myself all over, try to get her off me. Finally I'm free, except for the naughty talk intruding, still tainting my thoughts.

Food, eat. That'll put your feet back on the ground. Janet said I should eat something. It helps take your mind off errant thoughts, that's what she always tells me. Now Lana says she has something for me to eat. Something better than bagels.

Hummmmmm. Hum some more, drown her out. Okay, that's better. Leave me alone, please. I have to eat, then there's the *Atlantic* article.

The kitchen ceiling is a high one, ten feet, as I recall. Looking at it gives me vertigo. Pale, off-white paint with brown clouds. No, those aren't clouds. It's something else. The bathroom's overhead. Maybe Lana really did splash water onto the floor, and it's leaking down. A dark brown wallpaper valance strip, a vague, pale design on it at random intervals, outlines the walls at the ceiling. The pale stuff, something meant to portray clouds? I don't know, not for sure. There's a spread of tiny, ill-tempered robins, and some rosebushes covered with blood-red blooms.

Turn away, John, don't look at them. Yeah. Look at the wall cabinets; they're made of natural cherry. Good.

That's better. Janet loves cherry. The smell is so earthy. Go ahead, get a saucer and a cup. And you'll need cream. Sunlight edges through the big window to my left. So warm. Such a nice, safe space, except for that wallpaper, and whatever is on the ceiling.

Janet's left half a pot of coffee, but there're no bagels on the butcher block in the middle of the room, just a large wedge of cheese. My meds, there, in the amber plastic container, where the bagels should be. Take one, with orange juice. Ah. Bagels are in the fridge, behind this loaf of rye.

"If you take that caplet," Lana warns, her tone harsh, "I'll have to go away. I'll have to give it to some other guy. Do you want that?"

Brush her off, hands over your ears. Okay, she's gone. Goose bump-raising air swirls about me, takes my nervous heat over Lana away. Close the refrigerator, John.

That's it now, cut a bagel, put it in the toaster. Eat, and then see if you can muster enough energy to get the article moving. They smell so good, the bagel and coffee.

Janet left the newspaper scattered across our tiny maple dinette table, sunlight illuminating the news. Uh. Some parts of the paper are missing. Which? I separate out the remaining commercial dross, hold up the front section, and stir a spoonful of sugar into my coffee.

At last I'm sitting, relaxing, the sun warm on my back. A sunny glow pulses in every fiber of the crackling front page. The sunlight's so strong today. Odd. It tickles as I run my hand through it. It's mesmerizing, this glow. So full of life. Turn and follow it, John, back to its source.

Up the wall, the paper robins begin to wave, to flap their wings. They fan the sunbeams' heat, making it undulate like waves on the lake. Whoa. Robins don't really live in there. And look at their color, almost like dried blood.

It's a plot. The robins, are they trying to control me, too? No telling who, or what, might be buried in that soiled wallpaper. Come on, look out the window, where the light is, where everything's softer, less threatening.

The window, framed at the top by something Janet made of yellow linen, reaches almost to the ceiling. It stretches, keeps stretching, all the way to the sky. The sunlight's growing stronger. It floods through the panes and falls in dusty, tan rhomboids onto the floor tiles. Hold on, don't fall! Vertigo again.

A clack, from near the stove. My bagel halves look like a pair of thick, vertical lips, like…no, don't think about that. They're blueberry, the smell so captivating. Butter them, cover them with jam. Oh, that's good.

But the coffee, Janet's using decaf again, and it's way too strong, a lot stronger than yesterday. It's doctor's orders, she told me when she first started this. No stimulants, no caffeine, no alcohol. And I have to take my meds.

Right, the meds, forgot that. Pour the juice, take one, right now. You don't want trouble, do you? Swallow it, chase the juice down with the rest of your decaf.

Halfway through another cup, the paper's lead stories begin to make sense. Huh. Same stories as yesterday. And the day before. Threats of a new war in the Middle East. The military is beginning its run-up.

Then the research for the article takes over my thoughts, and the whole piece falls together in an instant. It's going to be so easy. I'll make my deadline this time. Maybe I'll finish the first draft today. Have to remember this stuff long enough to write it down, though.

Yaah! Turn the telephone ringer down. Don't know why Janet wants it so loud. Quick, before it rings again! Fumbling with this jangling wall thing makes me nervous. You never know who it'll be. Hope it's not my editor, wanting to exert pressure.

I bark a husky hello.

It's Ted. His asthmatic breathing rushes into the void between us. I can't make out what he's saying, but he sounds worried. He's probably expecting me to ask how he is. Or where he is. Or why he's run away. I should ask why he's gone off like this. No, if I do, it'll open doors. Better save that for later. The buzzing in my head ebbs, followed by clarity. Absolute clarity.

"I'm at Grandma's," he's saying. "She made me call."

Through his hand, a muffled conversation ensues, then another voice, female and strident.

"John?"

Oh, God. Don't talk to her. But you have to say something, or things will become awkward, very awkward. "Yes."

"Johnny, how are you, son?"

What can I possibly say? I mean, how can I relate anything to her? I've never been able to tell her how I am, what's wrong with me. "I don't know." My reply sounds like a tacit admission, a guilty plea. I have to counter, can't let her start in on me. "I'm all right," I add, trying to sound hopeful.

"Ted says, how did he put it, Johnny, you're freaking him out."

I conjure saliva, swallow until my throat's moist, mumble something inaudible, work a bagel crumb from between my lower lip and teeth onto my tongue, crunch it. My teeth are so rough against my tongue. What's this? Some strange, electronic noise that must be coming from the receiver. A faraway voice is telling me something, but what? No! Not another voice. Not now, not when I've just found Ted.

The old bat's voice rises. She's badgering me, the way she did when I was little. She's so strong-willed. Once again, her broad leather belt cracks across my back and legs. Echoes return of her terrible, banshee-like screeches, enumerating my various sins.

Dr. Blucher says I need to let my feelings out about her, it'll help everyone understand. But I know it won't. There's no credibility anymore. Janet, Ted, and this woman – they think I'm crazy, deluded, living in some outlandish world of my own creation. But I didn't create this; it's beyond my ability to dream up this sort of horror. If anyone created this, it's this old woman. She's trying to make me into her child again, after all I've been through with her. Control, that's it. She wants a little boy again, someone she can mold, the way she did me. Ted. He's next.

Freaking *him* out? The old bat is freaking *me* out. Have to tell her that. She's the demon here, not me. Come on, John, think it through. The meds are working. You can handle this conversation. I'm trying, but it's so hard. It's her haranguing and Dad's genetics. It's their fault. Dr. Blucher said so.

"Johnny, he says you refuse to bathe. He says you stay locked in the attic for days on end. You don't eat." A burdened sigh escapes her.

Oh, no. Here's the buzzing again, filling me, so I dash toward the den. She started it. All she has to do is call, meds or no meds, and I'm a basket case again.

I need to pace. Into the den. Uh oh. That must be Vince climbing through the den's west window, the window facing the lake. Just returned from the cliffs, he brushes a bit of dust from the arms and lapels of his coat with the backs of his hands. Then he combs back his auburn hair with one hand, pats it into place. He starts in, ever so politely, about how nice it is at the lake. I have to shut him out. Focus. What did the old bat say? Oh, yeah, food. You ate breakfast; you have her this time. Tell her.

"I just ate. A bagel. I had coffee."

She lowers her voice into that same, awful, familiar sternness. Vince, who seems quite dignified otherwise, apes the strong, almost masculine set of her jaw, the piercing blue eyes.

"Tell me you're not having caffeine again," she hisses, snakelike.

"Decaf. Janet makes decaf now." My hand's shaking in sync with the tremor in my voice. She hears it, all right. She knows, she always knows. She knows how to control me. And she's told everyone how to read my thoughts.

"Good," she says, her snaky voice evincing a pleased whisper. "Stay put, son. We'll be there in a couple of hours."

My hands are shaking so bad I can hardly hang the phone on its cradle.

"Well," says Vince. It's almost noon, and he's reappeared, standing before the couch, hands splayed outward at shoulder level, palms toward the ceiling. "That's that."

I nod, slump into the rocker. I've been in the attic working, at long last. Fifteen pages in one morning, can you believe it? My preliminary argument is finally set, tying the prospective new war in Iraq to the old one.

It's not oil, it's simple hegemony. That's my argument. We've always wanted to raise the flag over as much of the Middle East and Asia as we can before Russia or China beats us to it. Oil matters, of course, but the big thing's land, territory. With territory in hand, you can control the oil, the people. The messiahs of democracy, that's us. A new religio-political crusade, before the Russian and Chinese secularists make their next moves. Sure, the article will draw manic, ill-composed counterattacks, but that's the way it is these days. No rational ripostes, just mindless, dogmatic, emotional ranting.

But before I could compose a defense against whatever counter-arguments I might anticipate from this article, my meds began to wear off. The attic seemed suddenly dark. Its bare walls started collapsing in on me, something that's never happened before. So I closed out my file and lumbered down here, to the den.

I'm panting, my neck now sticky with sweat. "Yeah," I reply to Vince, "I guess that's that. For now. But I have to edit what I've written."

He chuckles and nods toward the door. "She's coming for a little visit, eh? You can handle it, my friend. She won't be here long, you know that. All you have to do is hold it together for an hour, maybe two."

I eye him, this my most recent visitor, the most lifelike, except for Lana, of course. He's a dapper little fellow, this time wearing a Panama hat over his graying hair, the hat's shadow deepening the spiderweb of wrinkles on his face. An orchid protrudes from one lapel of his white linen suit. Why are these people always so short, so fragilely built? If the doctor's right, that they're figments of me, they should be brooding hulks like me, right?

"Not at all," Vince remarks, leaning on his white-tipped, black-lacquered cane, one white-shoed foot across the other, toe to the floor, looking like a plantation owner version of Mr. Peanut. "Is everyone in the world the same size, the same temperament? Take that agent of yours — what was her name?"

"Pamela? Pam Harding?"

"Right," he says, nodding, "that's the one. Was she even remotely like you, in any way whatsoever?" He steps soundlessly forward, spins gracefully on the balls of his feet and settles into a prim pose on the couch's middle cushion. He eyes me, waiting.

Pam was the first of a succession of agents, most of them recent. But she was my best, the most energetic on my behalf. With my Master of Fine Arts diploma in hand, this house an inheritance from Janet's deceased parents – that tragic, horrendous disease from the tropics – I set up shop in the attic and began my first novel. In those days, my fiction ran in torrents from mind to fingers to computer file. If only the flow now would have that laminar flow.

"That's rot," says Vince. He uncrosses his feet, stands like he's about to attack. "The words still flow. You don't write them down, that's the only problem."

"Most of the time they don't make sense," I grouse. This acerbic posture of Vince's puts me on edge. Look at my clenched hands. My eyelids are twitchy.

"How would you know what makes sense?" he asks. "You think Joyce worried about that? You think someone with his Irish temperament would have been that insecure? Do you think a writer with a shaky ego could have written pages on end in that stream of consciousness form?"

"Sometimes my mind's not right for fiction," I tell him. "Meds, I have to take meds. I can't – it's hard to sustain a made-up world that long."

"Go ahead," he taunts, "take your medications, and see if that helps you write. They make you feel safe, that's all. You think real fiction writers are sane? You think the daemon reveals things to a sane person? No, John, to be truly inspired is to be insane in small, controlled doses."

Now we're getting to it. He's challenging me with the crux of my own argument regarding fiction.

"And anyway, do you really think readers want the same old sanity they're bludgeoned with at work, on TV, in magazines, day in and day out?"

He obviously revels in the uncertainty this stirs up in me. No, I need to stick with world affairs for now. Something concrete. Gather the facts, make the arguments. I'm weak, so weak when it comes to fiction. See? Just a few words from him, and I can hardly mount a challenge.

He gives me a knowing nod, his jaw set, the hint of a smile, his dark, squinting eyes expressing triumph. "That's what Pam meant. You're a bloody flake, John."

He's referring to Ted, but a very indirect reference. During Janet's pregnancy I was rewriting the difficult, middle chapters of my third novel, twisting the plot line one more time. For some reason, I got lost in my own convolutions, couldn't go farther. After a month of this wrestling, Janet went into labor.

At three in the morning, I called her obstetrician and hurried her to Humana in Lawrenceville. Things inside her were almost as twisted as my story, and it took a C-section to deliver our son.

Ruddy and wet, he seemed a miniature Janet, the wisps of red hair slowly coming unglued and beginning to curl. It might have been my imagination, but his splotched face carried her thoughtful but troubled pout. But one look into those blankly staring blue eyes and my story came together.

Another character, that was it! The convolutions I was wrestling with needed another character to show the way. Ted. Their child. Someone to disrupt their ideals, their pre-planned future, lead them in another direction.

Three weeks later, Janet and Ted had long since settled into their daily routine. Meanwhile, I'd worked this new character into my manuscript. Then Pam called.

"Just wanted to see how the rewrite is progressing," she said in her impatient singsong.

"You won't believe what I'm doing with it," I began.

"What?" she interrupted, the word red with alarm. "You know we have a publication date of September first."

Unable to resist a chuckle, I said, "Maybe, we'll see," knowing that would set her teeth on edge. "Everything's flowing now, but there's a change, a big one."

"The ending too?"

"Sure. How could I work these new elements in without changing the ending?"

Her sigh was almost a growl. "How long?"

"By the first week of October, for sure."

"You realize that would be a breach of contract."

So what's one more? I remember thinking. The writing had been phlegmatic from the start, almost a biological revulsion on my part, and it eventually groaned to a halt just prior to my original turn-in date. But obsession earned me a reprieve. I wanted to get it right, no matter the cost. Nine months later, the manuscript slowing again, I almost lost my contract. What was I to do? I couldn't turn in some mediocre piece of pulp, couldn't do that to my readers. No, I had to tough it out, try this and that, untie each knot until everything became a coherent whole. Finally it did, inspired by Ted.

At the time of this conversation, though, I could only laugh Pam off one more time, try to turn her in an upbeat direction. "If you say so. You have to realize, this is great, Pam. Everything's coming together, you'll see. It'll be worth the wait."

"Let me talk to Steve," she said, shoving her sentence into mine and hanging up.

I had to smile. Nothing to worry about. Steve Poss, my editor, he likes me. He'll back me up.

Pam called back an hour later. "I talked at length with Steve. He wanted to know if this is a whim. It's not a whim, is it, John?"

A whim? What is fiction if not a huge whim? "Well, I suppose not. The story was flat in the middle, as boring as a drive across Kansas. Didn't you tell me to spice it up?"

"I told him it's not a whim, that you'd thought it through. He said, 'I don't want to see this character create digressions I'll have to edit out.' I told him the truth, didn't I, John?"

We went over the changes together, and she slowly came around. But her tone with me changed in the ensuing days and weeks. More distant, cooler, as if she were distracted. My update calls seemed an unwelcome burden on her.

Steve had my manuscript in hand on October first, as I had assured Pam. Then came his flood of corrections: bad grammar, misspellings, awkward sentences. I was appalled. No MFA professor, no editor, had ever seen this lack of basics from me. But the changes came and went quickly. We made a mid-November publication date, in time for holiday sales, the book appearing on the New York Times bestseller list right after New Year's.

Pam dropped me six months later, telling me in her usual blunt fashion that the industry was beginning to see me as temperamental, unstable.

"A flake," Vince now reiterates. "You were becoming a flake. Looking back, you must see that."

See it? I simply took it in stride. With my first two books on every bestseller list, the first in paperback, Pam's dropping me seemed an unwarranted anomaly.

I signed then with Wade Barker and, before I was through with my first *Atlantic* article, he dropped me, saying he wanted to focus on his more productive writers.

As if I hadn't been. After all, there was travel to Bangladesh. Then the conflicting testimony from interviews about a surge in industrial pollution on the Ganges and Brahmaputra Rivers, and on the Hilsa prawn fishing in the country's delta region. Not to mention that fakir. He put a hex on me. I realize now that that's what happened to me, that's what's wrong with my head. The fakir.

"Excuses," Vince exclaims. He rises from the couch, strides over and pokes at me with the tip of his cane. His gaze is haughty, fearless.

A low rumble from the drive, and an engine stops. A car door slams.

Vince shrinks noticeably. He darts to a window overlooking the porch and yard, looks out, and hurries back. "We'll finish this conversation later," he says, his voice full of urgency. He steels himself and swallows, looks toward the door, then back. "But this one word I'll leave with you. Discipline. And I mean emotional." He strides to the window facing the lake, dives through it, and disappears.

The lights, John, switch on lights, the way Janet wants you to. Make everything as bright and clear and sane as possible. Sane. Huh. This isn't going to be sane. I can feel the odd tingling within me as the buzzing ups its volume. Feet clomp up the steps and across the porch floor, loud and determined steps alternating with quieter, timid ones. I tense, pull myself erect in the rocker, and stand. The door opens. Breath leaves me.

THREE

Ted enters first and stops, looking like a frail oyster pushed from the shell of the rangy, overly serious woman hovering behind him. Afternoon sunlight angles sharply in from the west, swipes at their spreading, gloomy shadow. The two move as one across the foyer and into the den's dim ambience. Nervous, hoping to deter any unannounced figments, I pull the switch cord to the floor lamp. Mom lets one of the lumpy plastic grocery bags she's carrying slip to the floor so she can flip on the ceiling light. Huh. Thought it was already on. At any rate, there's no room for imagination in this bright light.

Ted disengages from his overseer. His jeans are puckered at the waist, a belt end dangling. His white polo shirt is draped across bony, hunched-forward shoulders, and it's pleated more or less evenly into his jeans. All this makes him seem more like a pale, redheaded nerve end peeking from within the oyster's labia.

But his eyes – they're fascinating. Why haven't I noticed that pleading quality before? They're calling for help, like the ones I see in the bathroom mirror, the reflected confluence of fear, anger, and despair. Not a good thing to see in an offspring's eyes, but can't it be a good thing, too? Isn't a father supposed to see himself mirrored in his son?

His grandma, though – she's an alien creature, from a world totally unlike the one Ted and I inhabit. Her gray pantsuit is intended to complement the lopped-off, almost shoulder length salt-and-pepper hair. Instead, her outfit accentuates steely, slate blue eyes. The white blouse and pantsuit jacket covering those extraordinarily broad shoulders hang loosely, halfway to the knees, concealing a protruding tummy, her only true lack of vanity. Otherwise, there's no recess within to house the whimsical, the imaginative. She's a utilitarian, all business, no frills package.

She picks up the grocery bag and strides soldier-like toward me in an undeviatingly straight line. Her twill pant legs whistle, the flimsy plastic bags at the end of each arm swing like a pair of oversized fists.

No. Retreat. Don't come any closer! I almost trip over the rocker legs as I put the chair between us. The buzzing's back full-tilt, and it's rising in pitch. Hands over ears. That's no good – the buzzing raises a clamor, a ringing with a multitude of overtones, a thousand crazed voices singing off-key and laughing. Can't say anything, though; don't want her to know she affects me this way. One deep breath. Two. And one more for the Gipper.

"Oh, my God," she says, her loud, mannish voice rising to the room's cavernous ceiling and flooding down the walls to engulf me. She's stopped, the rocker between us. "Ted was right, Johnny, you reek." An expression of disgust frames her flared, offended nostrils.

My palms fly out in involuntary defense. They press the rocker forward a few inches. Then, despite realizing body language speaks for one's emotions, I plunge my hands deep into my front jeans pockets, my rebellious pose, the method I used to hide my feelings, when I was Ted's age. Why haven't I grown emotionally since then? Why do I have to react this way to old hurts?

"I took a bath," I announce. Unfortunate. My tone's more argumentative than I intended. This will probably set off another skirmish between us, escalating quickly and without hope of reconciliation.

The lamplight gains strength as the sun begins to slip toward a stand of pines and poplars at the periphery of our yard. The afternoon's first cooling breeze slips through the lake window and into the den. To my rear, the grandfather clock quivers out its seconds.

Mom's expression is skeptical. She huffs and then lugs her groceries to the kitchen. Returning, she circles us and flicks a long finger at Ted, directing him to the rocker. Without a notice or a word, he obeys. I turn the chair for him, shove it a body length away, and move to the couch's other end.

From the coffee table's opposing side, she leans toward me, her distaste grown more pronounced. Again, she sniffs. "You bathed? Then it's probably the clothes. Why are you wearing such filthy rags?"

An embarrassed shrug. Then my attempt at verbal defense tumbles out, incoherent noise filling the space between us. I want to explain that Janet has hid my good clothes, that maybe she's sold them. That's her way of keeping me here, locked up, a prisoner. I can't bring myself to tell Mom that, so my rejoinder goes unuttered. But why would Janet have done that? Well, she wouldn't. She's my angel, my guardian. Maybe it's best that my explanation came out a lexical jumble. Mom wouldn't have believed me. She's never believed me, about anything.

Ted shrieks, his feet scooting back and forth beneath the rocker, his nose in the crook of one elbow as he looks my way. "Jeez," he groans, "you're worse than yesterday, Pop. A lot worse." He's acquired an Adam's apple recently, and it bobs, a distraught cork on the surface of some inner agitation he's not yet willing to reveal.

Mom spins and glares. She reaches for him, as if about to clamp him to her, the way she used to do me. He shrinks deeper into the rocker. She's dominating again. She's bent on intimidation, on control. Not me this time: Ted.

She turns back to me, her thin-lipped glare softening. She scans me, uncritically for a change, inspects me from head to toe, as if a lab specimen. Her face creases fold deeper as her jaw clenches. She's made a decision.

She orders, "Get up, Johnny. We're going to get you dressed properly."

My guttural protest is too weak to seem rebellious. I rise as bade, head bowed, an embarrassed flush on my face. She strides toward the stairs and I follow, up all twenty-one of them, to Janet's bedroom.

She plunges into the closet, clothes hangers squeaking against their pole, while I wait in the bedroom doorway, rocking across the balls of my feet. She emerges, hands on broad hips, and says, "You have plenty of clothes, Johnny. Now get in there and pick something to wear."

I shake my head no.

"If you don't, I will."

Can't let her do that. Control. She wants control. So I take a deep breath and plunge in. Feeling, grabbing, then emerging, I display a pair of tan slacks, a blue dress shirt with a button-down collar, a black belt and shoes to match. She nods, and I lay them across the bed's rumpled, white-flowered blue comforter. As she's done of late, Janet's left the bed unmade. Mom grimaces, and I know it's her distaste for things undone, so I gather my clothes, pull the covers up one-handed, smooth and arrange them a bit. Once again I lay out the clothes.

My belt snakes away and snags on something below one of the uprights on the antique four-poster. Uh oh. How can I be sure it's really a belt?

As I'm taking this thing in, she turns and lunges toward our chest of drawers. Eyes on the snake, I barely notice her paw through one drawer, then another. I'm suddenly disjointed, detached, not sure of my intent, but I sense I'm moving, away from the snake. Finally, it resumes its belt-like form. A pair of black socks, a tee shirt and underpants have somehow appeared on the bed.

"Take off those rags," the hag commands.

"Now? Here?"

"Yes." Her voice is low, husky, insistent, exhibiting a clear threat. "Right here, in front of me. Now."

Shame. I'm five again, standing naked before her, as if a troublemaking toddler. That unrelenting gaze never leaves me. Then she steps forward, sniffs. Those flicking eyes dare me to move.

"All right," she says, "you did bathe. Put on those clean clothes."

So I sigh and pull on the underwear and socks, then the shirt, slacks, shoes, and belt.

"Into the bathroom."

I know what she wants. I locate my electric razor, sit on Janet's vanity bench. Tug after tug, the razor alternately cuts and pinches my whiskers. Should have used pre-shave lotion, but she was so insistent.

"Now the hairbrush."

She's so harsh. Looking up and into her narrowed eyes, I tug forcefully at the tangles. It hurts. Finally it's done.

"Turn to the mirror," she orders, "and look at yourself."

Who is this person? It could have been me a couple of years ago, except for the deeper facial divides and puffy cheeks, the graying temples, the orderly but too-long hair that's been pulled left and right. Something about this image appeals, but its core is now too alien for me. What if that other, scruffy, smelly version is the real me?

"This is how you look, Johnny, when you take care of yourself."

"I know." Does she think I'm some sort of fool, that I don't know how to groom myself, to dress properly, without her close-order instruction? But why should I bother? Why dress like this in order to huddle over a computer in my attic refuge, alone, day in and day out? And how did she find these clothes, anyway? It's as if she knew exactly where to look. Maybe she and Janet have been talking. Maybe they're conspiring. No, that's too weird to even contemplate.

"Son," she growls softly, her version of tenderness, "you have problems, we all know that. Janet's obviously of no use to you, so you must take hold of yourself. See how easy it is to do the basics?"

Easy for whom, her? She doesn't want to empathize, she has no inkling of the helplessness I feel, my life skating out from under me at every opportunity. It's always about her, for her. What does she know, or care, about how slippery my personality has become, how hard it is to negotiate each day? She wants to keep me from being an embarrassment, that's all.

Now she backs away and points to my dirty clothes. They do stink. I have to hold them away, between thumb and forefinger. She turns and stalks from the room, leaving me. All right. I know I have to wash these offending rags.

Downstairs, she's standing just off the foyer, before the alcove containing our washer and dryer, hands on hips again. I throw my clothes into the washer, along with some detergent, and twist the dial. A gurgle within the walls, and the machine begins its dark hum.

She glares, unmoving. "Johnny, please straighten yourself."

I've neglected to fasten my belt properly, to align shirt with slacks. She gives me an exasperated huff and strides toward the den.

We find Ted there, hanging up the phone. His wide-eyed look suggests a sheepish grin is forthcoming,

147

but it falters, taking on his more familiar, sullen, eyes-half-closed, teen-age outcast pose. He's saying something, but my buzzing overwhelms it.

"Ted, what?"

"He says he's just called Janet," Mom announces over Ted's mumbles. "She's leaving work. She'll be home soon." She sighs, glances at her wristwatch. "Take a shower," she barks at Ted.

"Okay," I repeat, "take a shower."

His head drops into his neck. He blinks. He wouldn't do this if it were my suggestion alone. In a single day, he's become dangerously subservient to this woman. He plods toward the stairs.

"Hurry," she calls after him, her tone noticeably less threatening, as if she's realized her excessive harshness. "I'm fixing lunch, and you won't want to keep your mother waiting." Then she strides toward the kitchen.

Alone at last. Deep breath, John, relax. The worst is yet to come, though; I can feel it.

Water coughs, then hisses within the upstairs walls as Ted begins his shower. Judging by the chopping sounds, the clang of pans, Mom's preparing homemade vegetable soup. Hope she'll let me have one of her tomato and Swiss cheese on rye sandwiches with that. Her cooking and food preparing – they're the only fond memories I have of childhood.

"Food?" whispers a voice. It's Ezra. "Feed your mind, your perceptions," he says, "that'll feed your body. Otherwise you'll be a fathead. Take it from one who knows."

I jump, startled. The pronouncement is so clear, so forceful, so near. Why can't I be that succinct?

"Where are you?" I whisper. My head swivels left and right, then ceiling to floor. He's been promising to reveal himself for several days. He has to. I hate these abstracted voices.

My meds, they're in the kitchen. Dr. Blucher said I could take an extra occasionally. Well, this is occasionally. I can't get to them, not with her in there. I can't.

"Look out the window, toward the lake," says Ezra. "You wanted to see me in tangible form, didn't you?"

"Yes. I mean, no. Go away! And take the others with you." That's posturing on my part. I don't want to admit they fascinate me.

He laughs. "All right, I'll shut up, if that's really what you want. But I'm telling you, I'm tired of this cloak and dagger stuff. I'm ready to come clean, open the raincoat and flash you, if you get my drift. But I'll go away. For now." Then he adds, "The others, though, you're the only one who can make them disappear. They won't pay any attention to me. Sorry, but I'm not the authority figure you are."

The voice pauses, and something tells me he's moved closer.

"Now," he whispers, "won't you please look toward the lake? That's where they are, if you want to tell them anything. Matter of fact, that's where we all are."

A rustling sound tickles both ears, actually more like a fluttering, maybe wings, maybe my heartbeat – and Ezra's gone. For now, as he says. Still, I can't help but peek through the west window.

What's this? Michael's grown larger. He and Lana are dancing, some sort of hoedown step. Someone else, a plump figure. Ezra, certainly, and clad in a blue Luftwaffe uniform, squints through a pince-nez. He's slicked back his hair in nineteen-forties fashion, a fiddle to his left shoulder. He hunches over it and saws away at the dance's melody, his strokes bouncing about the rhythm Lana and Michael are kicking up.

Carly, Lana's look-alike – her evil twin, Lana says – pats a foot and claps, tries to entrain the fiddle's erratic rhythm.

They're having so much fun. Why can't I, too?

"You can," a small, quiet voice tells me. "It's all out there. Later you can go with them. The lake, that's where the real action is."

Another voice? No!

"Johnny!"

The den reverberates with the leavings from Mom's muscular bellow. Talk about an icy bath.

"Do you want a sandwich?"

"Yes," I manage, barely above a whisper, "tomato and Swiss cheese. Did you bring some rye?"

"I've set out a wedge of sharp cheddar," she calls out. "And, yes, I brought rye."

My chest is so tight I can hardly breathe.

After a pause, she calls out again. "Have you taken your medication yet? I see you've left it here in the kitchen."

I want to tell her it's not quite time for one, but that's only a partial truth. But wouldn't that cancel the partial lie of it? I've always been a stickler for truth, whether I'm writing fiction or articles. But is truth the important thing right now? Am I living truth? No, not with these voices, these figments. Reply more truthfully, John. Put your best foot forward. "Now," I squeak. "I need one now."

"They're right here. And there's a half-finished glass of orange juice to take it with."

Best to stay here, though. Can't risk a trip to the kitchen. "Can…can you bring it?"

Her voice, which was momentarily filled with semi-motherly overtones, now turns cold. "I'm stirring the soup. Come get them. They're both here by the double sink."

"All right." The trembling I feel at my core works its way to my hands, my breathing, my gait. Slip in, slip out. Take the pill, wash it down, and then get the hell out.

As I enter, wisps of steam rise from the soup. It hisses quietly. But the cheese she's left out, warm but so rich and tart. Despite my edginess, I start making sandwiches. Janet, Ted, and I, we never have meals like this anymore. Is that my fault? We need to cook more, we need to do it for Ted. He needs the nourishment. I mean, look at the kid. He's skin and bones.

A pair of sandwiches done, I manage to cross her territory, take the pill and escape. I settle into the rocker and glance to the window, expecting the dance party to be peaking, but there's nothing. No one. That's a good sign, isn't it? Doesn't it mean I'm not creating figments? Anyway, that sort of diversion – okay, temptation – doesn't work well with Mom around.

A clomping on the stairs. Ted. The footsteps are buoyant this time, more self-assured. It's amazing what a shower can do if you don't listen to its seductive mutterings.

The buzzing has stopped. My thoughts have calmed, slowed, peaceful spaces between them. The medication's working, at least a little. It's hardly been ten minutes.

Ted has put on clean jeans and a pale blue polo shirt. He circles the couch, quietly, eyes flitting timidly toward me. "You look nice," he says, without expression.

"Thanks. You, too." Maybe there's something to this bathing and clean clothes business. Maybe hygiene is good for the soul.

Ted, he's open to a little bonding, I can feel it. The time's right. But can I pull it off? We haven't had much to say to each other lately.

"I'm glad you're back," I tell him. "You okay now?"

He braces himself, eyes me cautiously. A smile inches its way onto him. "I'm okay."

"Good. That's good. Maybe we can talk some."

I want to say more. So many things have occurred to me. Insights. Regrets. Come on John, open up.

Sorry, no can do. It's there, on the tip of my tongue, but it refuses the light of day.

Head bowed, he waggles a foot. "Maybe later. I'm going outside. I'll be on the porch for a while."

"All right."

He scurries to the door, flings it open, bangs it shut. The house fills with the slam's reverberations.

A noisy, ceramic clatter rattles the kitchen. The soup must be almost done; Mom's setting out bowls. It's going to be so good, having a meal like this again. I lick back the saliva escaping one corner of my mouth. Another good sign. Usually my mouth is so dry.

Ted's on his vigil, so I turn to the television. First click takes me to CNN. U.S. armored divisions are massing on the southern Iraqi border, in Saudi Arabia. Then the report switches to Turkey, then Kurdistan, Iraqi soldiers preparing to defend their northern oil fields. An aircraft carrier in the Mediterranean launches one plane after another, bombing key positions along the main routes to Baghdad.

This is good. TV will air important details, ones I'll need to complete the *Atlantic* article. Hope I can get back to it before I lose the morning's momentum. Maybe Mom will go home after lunch.

But Ted. Oh, man, Mom's up to something. This is going to be complicated. I can feel it.

On CSPAN, a Congressional caucus critical of the rationale for war begins a session in the Capitol basement. Its chairman, trying to stifle his emotions, speaks about the need for worldwide consensus in justifying the war. He doesn't think there are weapons of mass destruction in Iraq, the war's necessity yet to be demonstrated. He drones on about Shi'ite and Kurdish factions that may yet overthrow Saddam, that the vaunted Republican Guard is underfed and under-armed, that Guard morale is low. Our coalition's military should merely apply pressure externally, he counsels, and let internal Iraqi forces take over. Let world opinion against this awful man make his demise imperative from within.

On CNN again, a reporter challenges the Vice President with questions concerning the need for war. He laughs in an offhand way, spins out a well-rehearsed list of the administration's rationales.

What's that? A car driving up? Oh. There's Janet's voice – I can't make out what's being said, but the words are happy. As she and Ted talk, though, anger and hurt work their way into her tone. But she'll be okay now that he's back. Maybe now she won't give me that look. You know, as if I'm some sort of irresponsible freak, as if I'm the one who scared him into running away.

Janet and Ted bounce in, Janet laughing. Ted's smiling.

Mom hears the noise and strides into view from the kitchen. What's this? She's smiling, too. "You're just in time," she says to Janet. "Lunch is ready. Come to the kitchen, and we'll catch up."

"The war," I complain. "Let's eat in here. I need to see this."

Ted waves a fistful of mail, which he drops on the coffee table. "Mr. Rybicki, he picked up the mail for us."

Huh. He does that sometimes.

"Yes, let's eat here," Janet says, eying Ted, knowing full well the old lady's going to rake us both over the coals regarding our son. She examines me from head to toe. Is it that she doesn't believe I've cleaned up? Or does she like me better with the smelly clothes and unkempt hair? "We all need to take an interest in these awful events," she adds.

Mom's smile fades to hardness, ice in her eyes. "We need to talk, as a family, Janet, and we can't do that if I have to compete with the television." She sighs, scowls, orders me to bring the sandwiches in. "Come give me a hand," she says to Janet. "We're having soup, too."

Janet subtly mirrors Mom's scowl and sighs, knowing the "if I have to compete" stuff means a sermon, not a conversation. She swoops near me, lets out another breath, allows a light-as-air, momentary pressure of her breasts on my shoulder, brushes me with a kiss. She glides away. So desirable.

Oh, yeah, the TV. Another click brings me to the History Channel, a tableau materializing there of U.S. military might during the first Persian Gulf War. A voice describes the rows of armored vehicles the camera has taken in – Abrams tanks, armored personnel carriers, Humvees – they stretch in mind-boggling numbers across waves of desert dunes.

The camera shot darkens, the next one revealing suited-up soldiers, looking like robots out of *Star Wars* in their body armor, their hot, heavy, chemical warfare outfits, their packs and weapons.

A voice describes the formidable Iraqi bunkers coalition forces attacked in that war, now twelve years in the past. The bombs, the voice proclaims, won't destroy the bunkers. They'll kill those inside with concussive force.

Desert temperatures there will reach the 120s during daytime, the voice goes on. A view inside a huge tent reveals thousands of cartons of bottled water for the troops. Yet another voice-over details the soldiers' daily water and mineral losses.

The narrative introduces the earlier war's Allied commander, who begins describing to the press the effects of the day's bombings. He's a stout man, erect, proud, confident in manner. After a few more comments, he begins to bluster about Iraq using downed U.S. pilots as human shields against the bombings.

He winds down, picks up a pointer and announces to the crowd that they're about to see the luckiest man in Iraq. Lights in his bunker dim and a film begins, taken from an attack plane's vantage. The plane has just dropped a laser-guided bomb, a bridge its intended target. A truck races madly across the bridge. Seconds seem hours as the press corps waits breathlessly, the truck nearing the bridge's opposite end.

"And now, in his rear-view mirror," the general intones. An eye-blink later, the bomb reduces the structure to rubble and smoke, and the truck flees from view. Laughter and a scattering of applause rise from the reporters. The general gives the camera a wry smirk and nods to an aide, who adds more assault details.

"Can't we at least turn the sound down?" Mom asks. She must've set this overstuffed sandwich beside me. I forgot the soup, but that's okay. Ted and I, we'll be happy with just a sandwich.

I mute, still captivated by these images. Bombs are being guided to their targets as if on wires, some gliding perfectly into air vents, smokestacks, and assumed weak spots in bunkers, others demolishing bridges and roadways.

I can only guess at my attraction to this. Every explosion, every target destroyed, relaxes something inside me. Maybe it's the appeal of intent, forcefully applied, its aim unerring, focused, always successful. For the first time in days, something within me equates to peace.

My eyes glued to the screen, I hear Mom and Janet talking in the most casual manner. A commercial break interrupts the programming. Time to twist the rocker and face the music.

Janet's on the couch, running tongue over teeth, mouth closed. Ted's at the couch's opposite end. His sandwich plate's on the coffee table, atop the mail, the sandwich uneaten. He wedges himself into a corner cushion. Mom, rigid as the straight-backed cane chair she's sitting on, faces them from the coffee table's opposing side. Janet leans, guides a hand toward Ted's curls. He smiles, then goes grimly taut. Her hand stops.

"Honey," she coos, "why didn't you talk to me? When we couldn't find you, I didn't know what to do. I was so afraid."

He sneaks a glance Mom's way and his mouth opens, as if to speak. Instead, he gulps and shakes his head.

"Go ahead," Mom urges, "tell them what you told me. Tell them why you showed up at my door."

"All right," I urge him, "talk."

He blinks, gasps in a breath. He says nothing.

"If you don't tell them, I will." An edge has revealed itself in Mom's voice, one I remember from my childhood, threatening as it demands. She leans toward him, the move meant to enforce the threat.

He swallows, clearly frightened, eyes flicking left and right. What's he frightened of, Janet and me? Mom? Or is it something else, something he's reluctant to allow access to the light of day?

He glares at me, says, "I hate this. I hate it here." His tone is a snarl, so much more vehement than I would have thought possible from our moody son.

Silence fills the space between us. Then a thump from the window. A hummingbird has flown into the screen and slid to the ledge. It shakes violently, staggers to its feet, begins to vibrate, and flits away.

"What's wrong, Ted?" Janet's voice bleeds with hurt. She's on the verge of crying. "Don't you know how much it hurts me to hear you say such things?"

"I think that's part of the problem," Mom says, measuring her words, twisting visibly as she struggles to keep her cool.

I know her so well; she's determined to encourage some sort of encounter here, yet remain in the background. She won't, though. She's not a background operator. Has to stir things up, whip them to a froth, try to make each of us an extension of her ego. Go on, Mom, if you must. Start stirring.

She waits, says nothing, watches, Janet's inner hurt surfacing to tears.

"I know what you think," Janet exclaims after a throat clearing, a stanching of tears. "You think John's problems are at the root of Ted's."

"It doesn't matter what I think, Janet. And your telling him his opinion hurts you won't solve a thing. Ted has views on his home life, and he deserves to be heard. Your child's future is at stake here, as well as that of your marriage. Certainly you realize that."

What? Our marriage is at stake? How does she figure? She changes tack slightly, and her ensuing spiel concerning family dynamics is so predictable I could recite it with her. Would that life were as straightforward as she makes it out to be. This is her opening gambit in a master plan to run our lives, the situation she's always wanted, the eventuality Janet and I have never allowed. Ted's given her the opening she needs, though, and she can't wait to start pulling strings. All right, let's see what you have up your sleeve, old woman. Lay it out there.

Janet turns to Ted. She knows, as I do, not to be drawn too deeply into Mom's machinations. She knows to tread carefully. But this time she forsakes caution and plunges in. "Is she right, honey? How do you see things here?"

He continues to ignore her, still staring at me. "It's just that, like, you're so screwed up, Pop." The words come out as if under pressure, his voice rising to a pubescent squeak. "I wish I was eighteen so I could leave. If I could do that, I'd never come back."

Janet's eyes are red neon, lubricated with a continuum of tears. "Johnny, please do something."

It's amazing how dry your mouth and throat can become without noticing. But I have ideas on this. I just need to verbalize them before they slip away.

A laugh from my left ear, so loud I jump. "Are you sure you want to do this?" Ezra asks. "There's safety in silence, you know."

My response, barely an impulse of thought, replies in Elvis Presley's velvety singing voice, "It's now or never."

Ezra joins in, singing a passable harmony. He laughs as we repeat the thought-sentence over and over. Finally, in the tone of a TV news anchor, he replies, "Now back to you, John."

I need to wet my whistle. Maybe the soup. But it's probably cold by now, its taste gone. My appetite is, for sure. The buzzing, is it back? Yes, it's there, but distant, for the moment.

"You think I'm crazy," I reply to Ted. "You're ashamed."

Anger begins to glow behind Janet's tears, her wild, bleary look once more turned to our son. "He's your father, Ted, and he has an illness. He's trying. We're all trying."

He ignores that and shouts, "See? That's what I mean. You don't think there's anything wrong with you, and that's why it's so hard to make you take your medicine. You're filthy, every day you're filthy. You're a filthy, fucked up mess. You're not going to change at all."

"Don't indulge Ted like that, John," Mom warns. "And he shouldn't be allowed to use that sort of language."

Janet turns sparking eyes toward Mom, something I've never been able to do. Look away, that's always been my plan, avoid her. Run, if possible.

"Now look here," Janet says, "this is between Ted and John and me. We don't need your interference." She blinks her eyes' sheen away and sniffs. "We've always tried not to let occasional bad language inhibit communication between us."

Mom's response is cold, practiced, a manner she's long since perfected. "Well, Janet, it appears such latitude hasn't worked. And regarding my interference, as you call it, Ted wouldn't be here if I hadn't stepped in. Did he run to you with his troubles? No. He had a friend drive him to Augusta, to me. Either stop avoiding this, making excuses and shifting blame, or he's going back to Augusta."

"How dare you!" Janet bolts from the couch, leans across the coffee table toward Mom, fists clenched at her side, arms bent at the elbows, as if she's about to dive into the old goat.

The buzzing becomes most palpable. I have to do something while I can.

Ezra again. What's he saying? "All right people," he calls out, and the image is of a movie director. "Quiet on the set," he roars in a ludicrously gruff tone. "Ready? Roll."

I wriggle upright, lean forward. The words tumble from me, an avalanche of thoughts, pent up for years, on raising children.

Then it's time to take on Mom. I look her way, but that's dangerous, so I take the easier route and turn toward Ted. "You've never had the benefit of counseling," I say to her, "but I have. Given the way you are, you would've benefited from it, you really would." I choke on the dryness in my throat and have to stop. I want to tell her she could have had it right after Dad died. But she was too proud, too self-controlled to accept that she needed help. Her motives toward Dad had probably been well intended, but did she have to be so hard on him? Did she have to badger him so about his depression, as if it were a motivational issue? Didn't she see she caused more harm than good? Lick your lips, John, get it out there, once and for all.

"Look at the way I've always been around you," I go on. "I never felt I had the latitude to express my true inner feelings. You've always been so critical whenever I tried." I still can't fix my eyes on her. This is so hard. Head hanging, I plow on. "I've always felt that if I were to please you, I had to excel in everything. Everything."

That brings up another of those nasty memories, one I've shoved into my darkened recesses. I still have a diary she made me keep, accounting for every minute of every date I went on. The next day she'd critique the girl, what we did, how much time we spent doing this and that.

Now she's grinding her molars, jaws sawing. Janet's back on the couch and once more in tears, Ted gaping, as if struggling to comprehend. This is good.

We've never let our hair down as a family like this before. Okay, I realize these issues aren't the kind to disclose with a child around. The role of parents demands strength, solidity, wisdom, seriousness of intent.

Wait. I'm starting to sound like Mom.

A glance up. Her glare is so menacing. Keep your eyes on the floor, then go on. "All you've ever done is look for mistakes I've made. You never wanted the real me to surface, did you? Don't you see, that was always the problem. I couldn't be perfect, because I inherited a genetic weakness. From Dad. That's what you have a problem with – an innate, structural weakness, the one thing neither Dad nor you nor I could do anything about."

What, no reply? Mom and Janet hold blank expressions. Ted sits wide-eyed, mouth slack, stunned. Time seems to have stood still. A glance to the west window leaves me with a clear view of a glorious sunset. Its florid highlights swirl, fighting against darkness. But the encroaching night wins, gorges on the sun's colors. I think I'm beginning to understand the draw of the lake, the spectacle the cliffs offer at this time of day.

Dad – I've never been brave enough to defend him like this before. How alone he must've felt, no one to comfort him, Mom his taskmaster, I too young, too weak to be a factor. But sanity rules for the moment. Make the most of it, John. No time to revel. All right, if you must revel, then revel in the truth.

"And Dad," I go on, voice rising, hardly taking time to draw a breath. Don't want to lose momentum, the inspiration that's possessed me. "It wasn't depression that killed him. It was pressure, harping on his every failing. When it became too much, he sat on that toilet with a razor blade and killed himself. He *had* to slit his wrists, don't you see? That had to be his final act. But he didn't want to blame anyone. The letter he wrote? He kept repeating that one sentence over and over. 'It's not your fault. It's not your fault.'" A sigh. Dad committed suicide so he wouldn't have to confront her, her complicity in his despair. He did that for her. "Do you want to kill me? If you don't watch it, that's what you'll do."

Strangely, she still hasn't interrupted, maybe because she's never been talked to this way. She screws her face into a tortured pout. Then, on the verge of tears – a first, if not feigned – she pulls herself erect.

"Is this what therapy has done to you, Johnny? Taken your lack of discipline and personal responsibility and made you turn on me?"

Always a good move on her part. Take something I'm doing to help myself and make me feel guilty about it. But I have a riposte on the tip of my tongue. No, it's gone. That's okay, though; I've pretty much said it all. Anyway, my chin's trembling, eyes ready to spew tears, pent up over decades. Dr. Blucher told me saying this would make me feel better, but it hasn't. Somehow it seems vicious and uncalled for.

"There!" Janet shrieks, "John's said what we both feel. Now leave us alone to work this out."

Mom sniffs, dabs at the corner of her mouth with a knobby knuckle, exhales, and straightens. Resolute, always so resolute. "Ted came to me, Janet. Not to you, and not to Johnny. He's no longer comfortable here. He wants a better life than you can give him." She leans toward Ted, gives him an encouraging nod. "Tell them, son."

Ted's eyes are flitting wildly. His breathing is coming and going in punctuated gasps. He doesn't want to go with her, anyone can see that. He's trapped, the way I felt back then. He's confused, doesn't know what to do, and she's taking advantage of it. Then his chin falls to his shirt, his hands a pair of antsy snakeballs. He's completely consumed by her forcefulness. "I'm going to leave," he mumbles. "That's the best thing for me."

"Say it louder dear," Mom prods, "so they'll know you mean it."

He looks up, eyes full of panic. He shakes his head, says nothing.

"Goddamn it," Janet screeches, "leave our son alone! Just go home, please, and let us work this out with Ted."

Ever the stone-faced pillar, Mom says, "No, Janet, I won't go without Ted. Do you plan to take care of him the way you've taken care of my son?"

A severe, prolonged silence settles in, polar fields of electricity that threaten to disconnect us forever. I pick up the TV remote. Do they want these histrionics? Do I? No. I just want to make everything better.

On CNN again, the older Gulf War is about to end, and someone's talking in the background. I edge the sound to a barely audible level. The buzzing's rising again. It's hard to make out what Mom and Janet are saying, but I think it's about me this time.

A montage begins on TV, images hurrying by, as if embarrassed that this twelve-years-ago war happened, the medium looking for a place to hide the evidence. A SEAL team, nodding, self-assured, prepares gear, checks weapons. Bombs fall, buildings disintegrate. The oil fires begin. Iraqis surrender by the hordes. The two four-star generals, dressed in crisp, starched fatigues, shake hands and make nice for the cameras. A parade, down Constitution Avenue.

A segue to hospitalized American troops, gaunt, eyes like Ted's, darting, seeking some sort of escape from their situation, I imagine. They've apparently been told to smile, but the upturned lips are weak, empty. They try to shrug off the lesions, the shaking limbs the camera reveals. After this, a Pentagon official presides over a press conference, denies the existence of something the media are calling Gulf War Syndrome. Then a final segue, to Baghdad, the camera taking in children picking through the city's bombed-out rubble.

"Better turn it off for now," Ezra tells me in a hoarse whisper. "You're being paged."

Ted's expecting something, dreading it at the same time. I know the feeling.

"John," Janet pleads, in tears, "please do something. Are you going to let her take Ted from us?"

Somehow their conversation registered while I was watching TV. Mom has said something about my filthy clothes, Janet giving her a list of reasons, rational ones, for not setting out clean ones, for not badgering me to bathe, for ignoring my need to take medications.

Is this true? I thought she was simply frustrated and didn't know how to be of help. She's seen a counselor, she says, something else I didn't know. She's been told to allow me as much autonomy as possible in dealing with my condition.

Ted's standing now. His eyes are red and swollen, his cheeks flushed. He looks to the west window, approaches it. He leans back, against the sill, stares at the floor, shakes his head, and rakes a shoe back and forth. Then he eyes me before he glances over his shoulder, toward the lake. He knows the voices are calling me from there, and he's trying to interdict it.

Ezra's voice is faint, telling me it's something else. It's distance Ted wants, more distance from the mother and grandmother conflagration blazing about him. He's looking for an out. Hope he finds it. I certainly haven't.

"All right," Mom sighs. She rubs her flanks and then her knees, a sign she's taking a new tack. "Ted tells me he needs clothes —"

"Yes, all right," Janet shrills. "I admit it, we have a money problem. John hasn't been paid for his last two articles, and he has medical expenses. My salary –"

"I'm aware of your predicament," Mom interrupts, grinding the words out, reminding me of a bulldozer, a panzer tank. "I'm taking Ted to the mall to buy him a few things. While we're gone, I want you and Johnny to take some time to discuss what's transpired here, to make your peace with what's going to happen next." One corner of her mouth lifts in a sneer. "Without my so-called interference."

Ted's face drops into a scowl, suddenly disapproving of Mom's heavy-handed tactics. Well, that makes three of us who don't like the drift of Mom's flinty threats.

"We'll not be engaging in any fantasy shopping, though," she scolds Ted. "Just a few things to help you look presentable at school." She rises, turns, gives him her most menacing, controlling look. The scolding continues: "You told me you want to be treated like an adult, Ted, so drop the scowl. Don't act like a brat."

Wow. If I'd said that, for whatever reason, Janet would've been all over me. Even now, there're sparks in her eyes. She's holding her tongue, probably to forestall another firefight with this old master of intra-family combat. But even from my diseased point of view, it's clear Janet, or maybe both of us, has always doted too much on Ted, been too protective. So now he doesn't know what to do or what to expect from her. And I give him nothing at all. Oh, well. At least with Mom, he'll have consistency. He'll know the rules. All of them.

Mom extends an arm toward Ted and wiggles her fingers. He lurches from the window, mumbles, glances my way. She tries to gather him in. He ignores her completely.

She sniffs, turns to Janet and me. "I'm planning to stay for the night. I hope the two of you are comfortable with that."

"Sure," Janet replies, jabbing at Mom with her chin, a stubborn pose I know so well. "The guest room's clean, and the bed has fresh linen. I think you'll find it up to your standards."

Another wow. Janet has just pulled off a bit of sarcasm I'd never have had the nerve to try. Maybe Dr. Blucher was wrong; maybe the encounter needed is between these two women, not Mom and me. Maybe familial sanity lies somewhere between their viewpoints, not involving me in the least. I'll bring that up next week, at my session.

Mom eyes Ted, nods toward the door, signaling their exit. He glances my way one last time, lets out an anguished cry, races past her and out the door. She follows, yelling. At last, she's gone. But Ted's gone, too.

FOUR

"Damn her," says Janet. Her face is splotched red, and she's trembling. She's somewhere between rage and despair. Unable to contain her inner discord any longer, she moans, "We can't let her take Ted away, John. We have to do something."

"I know." I move to the couch.

She edges away, just far enough to recoup her mood and survey mine. What does she see? How do my inner fractures appear on the surface? Is she reading fear and anxiety writ large? Her eyes are blue seas in a universe of white, her lips parted, expecting…what? I suppose she thinks because I've formed a few coherent sentences I can do something about Ted.

What's this? Now she's beaming. "I'm so proud of you, John," she says.

Without my noticing, she's undone one of my shirt buttons, the one I've been toying with. She does such things without realizing it, I think. She's a bit unstrung at times like this, and she works it out through jitters. But does she know what this fidgeting is doing to me, what's bubbling to the surface? Wow. So enticing.

"You've never stood up to her that way before," she goes on. "Did you see the look on Ted's face?"

We're sitting, our feet together; they're the point of a mutual triangle. Ted was nervous, on edge. Predictable, I guess. That's the way I used to react to Mom's dictates.

"Scared," I reply with a nod.

She gurgles and bends forward, allowing a mote of glee to grow. "Scared? Well, you didn't see what I saw, then. That rebellious sneer he's always giving us? He turned it on your mom, full force." Now she laughs, loudly. "If she can cure him of that, well…"

It was more of a scowl, as I remember. And surely she doesn't mean this the way it sounds. Must clarify. "We don't want him to go. We can't let that happen."

Startled, she comes erect, peers into me. There's no reason for her to look at me that way. What have I done?

"Uh, oh," says Carly.

No, don't let it be Carly. She's worse than Lana, much worse.

"You said a no-no," chortles Carly. "Now you're in big trouble."

"I didn't say that," Janet says, her face puckered to a pout. The damned buzzing drowns her next sentence.

"She can't legally…" Janet wanders through her thoughts. "There's no way…"

What is it I'm sensing here? Janet really does want Ted to live with Mom? That's it, isn't it? I'll bet she's been planning this, talking to Mom without my knowing.

"If you want her to be on board, there's always the tried and true," Carly whispers conspiratorially. "Janet's a sucker for affection." She howls at her version of a joke. "Sucker!" she howls, "Get it? She's the sucker, or is it you, John? Can't tell the sucker without a program."

Ah, I think I know what Carly's getting at. This state of being washed and properly clothed makes me bolder regarding my needs. Hand extended, I lean into the void between Janet and me. A smile works its way to the surface, a tender, inviting one, I hope.

She stops talking and pulls her hands to her chest. Her jaw drops. She's incredulous. She's not expecting this. Then she offers a tentative, questioning smile in return and allows me in close. Her back gives under my hand's air-light pressure, my other hand finding its way into those weightless red ringlets bouncing across her shoulders.

We kiss. It feels like a long, deep, passionate one. Now our hands are flying. I'm inflating like crazy now, throbbing, the way I do when Lana trash talks. It's going to happen this time, I know it! I'm going to take her, right here, on the couch. Oh! Strawberries and cream! Careful, John, don't hurt her, she's so delicate.

Our clothing's in disarray, half on, half off, hands seeking, going everywhere and nowhere. Oh, God. It's been so long, too long.

She giggles. "Not here. It's not dark yet. The lights are on and the shades are up."

"Yeah." That's all I can say, lummox that I am. "Yeah."

Grabbing handfuls of clothes to keep them from falling, we waddle, groping, to the stairs. No, don't count them this time, John, climb, to the top, the landing dark as a tomb.

In the bedroom, and despite my oafish fog, we're all over each other, peeling away remaining clothes items as if so many disguises over a hidden truth. Now we're in her bed, our bed, just the bathroom light on to illuminate her alabaster skin, the unruly triangle of strawberry wool she's pushing toward me.

Oh. That damp, soft skin, part of it cool, the best part warm. That's it, nice and easy.

Uh. I'm dizzy – everything's revolving, like a carousel. She's screaming. We're panting. Pushing. I'm a rumbling Vesuvius, about to launch a moon shot. Five, four, three... Now I'm afraid, want to crawl in, all the way, be a baby again. Duck, Saddam! Missiles firing, bombs falling, buildings exploding.

We're still attached, twisted together, like the tiny fibers of her red ringlets. We roll, kiss, embrace. Luckiest man in...what, where? My head's so light, can't help the laughter. Buford, that's it. Luckiest man in Buford. Georgia. USA.

There's more, but I can't describe it. What is it I'm feeling? Off somewhere, in the wild blue, Lana and Carly whining in my ears. No, it's not them, its Janet. What's she saying? Oh, baby, oh, baby, evan, even, something like that, catcalling, trash-talking. Lewd, suggestive sounds, meaningless to anyone else, but to us it's passion. Fusion. That's it, fusion.

Janet groans, we fall apart. She's giggling again. Suddenly she bolts upright, straddles me, a long, tense seriousness overtaking her. Her mouth drops open, as if there's some forgotten thing she needs to express, but can't. Her jaw clenches shut. That look. What is it? What does she want to tell me?

"You know, John," says Lana. "You know."

It's shame, or is it guilt? Perplexity, maybe, I don't know.

"Don't think so hard, baby," Lana coos in my ear. "You'll figure it out. It'll come."

"He's mine," says Carly, startling in her vehemence, as if there's a battle going on between these two.

But what am I in all this, just some inert pleasure vehicle for two figments and a wife? Why is everything so disconcerting all of a sudden? It shouldn't be. Doom. It's doom I'm feeling. That's never been there before. No! Don't want to think, don't want to analyze.

One of my hands molds itself to Janet's face. She smiles, weakly. That look again, what is it? This isn't the way it's supposed to be post-coitus. There should be no danger signals, no doubt, just a trustful, complete after-merging.

At my periphery, these two figments – talking, laughing. Am I really that crazy? What's she thinking?

Maybe I'm not gauging her correctly. Hell, John, you never gauge anything correctly. Just the writing. Just the writing. Sometimes, anyway. Shut up, John. Shut up, Lana, shut up, Carly. Just shut up!

"I need to shower again, baby," Janet whispers. "Get dressed. They'll be home soon."

Watching her swivel naked into the bathroom is so nice, so reassuring. So grounding. Don't worry about these damp, sticky sheets. Even the water's hiss seems benign this time, a happy, playful, childlike laughter. I can even see the water stream flooding over her. It tickles, cascades over her feet, gurgles into the pipes. That's what water does, right? It cleanses, it purifies. It takes away barriers, eviscerates doom.

"You bitch!" Carly screams after Janet.

"Leave her alone, sister dear," Lana cautions, her tone big sisterly. "John has a lot to contend with. More than he realizes at the moment."

"He's up for grabs," Carly counters. "Don't you know what that means? He's not hers anymore, and he damned sure isn't yours. I want him, and I'm going to have him!"

What are they talking about? Usually there's a subliminal sense to the chatter between these figments.

That's what Dr. Blucher tells me. There's something we want to keep hidden when these people materialize out of…what? Thin air. Imagination. That's probably it. Imagination. They let us in on some dark thing in a way we can accept. Man, what a crummy way to live.

The water's stopped. Janet's humming. She's happy. That's good.

"Not as good as you might think," Lana whispers. "Use your imagination, John. Come to your senses before it's too late."

But fatigue is taking me. It's hard to think now. The medications, so depleting. Everything's so depleting. So complicated. Need rest. Sleep. I barely hear Janet slip through the bathroom door, rattle hangers in the closet, then the half-grunts, the half-stumbling of her dressing.

Her breathing, she's nearby. She's leaning over me, testing. She wants to see if I'm asleep. I am, I think. My breathing begins a low growl. Can't move. She's smiling, I know she's smiling, happy to see me at peace, even for a moment, satisfied I'm able to sleep.

There's a quiet click. I think she's picked up the phone, followed by soft steps across the room. She must be sitting on her vanity bench. The phone's flat chirping tells me she's pressed in a number. Hushed, intimate words. Can't make them out. Asleep. For real this time.

Sleep is so liberating. No more Lana or Carly or the others. No more Ted or Mom or Janet. Just freedom. Go where you want. I'm falling, down a mole hole, the past hurtling toward me.

Now the sun's out. Music playing. I'm on a walkway, mown grass all around. A dog, a terrier, barks and leaps. He grabs something. Ah. A Frisbee. I'm laughing, because I recognize where I am, what's about to happen. This is Piedmont Park. It's June, and Janet and I are going to be married today.

The park, Atlanta's central gathering place for over a century, is a dazzling, impressionistic montage of background cityscapes, oak greenery, blue skies and people. Laughter and birdsongs are everywhere. A red, orange, and yellow-striped hot air balloon is swinging over the skyline. Just past noon, and it's growing warm under the tree canopy. The morning's remaining cool wriggles upward and begins to dissipate.

Phil, my best friend, now a professor of American Lit at Emory University, the one who introduced me to Janet, stands to my right. He's talking low, cracking jokes.

I'd forgotten how dashing he looks in that gray, tailed tuxedo, jet-black hair hanging stylishly over the collar. It's a bit amusing for me to see this sun-browned soccer-playing, scholar-athlete nervous and jabbering away.

Less than a hundred yards ahead, at the end of the walkway, stands a gazebo. Within its open frame, a string quartet is playing, something by Handel, as I remember. Three rows of folding chairs have been arranged in an arc straddling the walkway, and almost all are occupied. There's Mom, sitting by Aunt Carol. Janet's mom and dad, her three sisters. The rest are friends, most of them paddling the air with wooden-handled cardboard fans. Some glance back, past us, craning for a first view of the bride.

Phil eyes me and says, "What's the holdup?" He tugs at his bow tie, wipes sweat from one bushy eyebrow. "We need to get you two to your love shack before dark."

We're to honeymoon in Highlands, in the mountains of North Carolina, a beautiful, bucolic trysting place. I have to chuckle. "So, Phil, you have money on something, or what?"

The Italian temperament he inherited from his mother is about to surface. He wants to give me a big bear hug, but he knows it's inappropriate. Instead, he punches my shoulder, that big paw almost knocking me off the walk. "I have fantasies, bro," he confides with a wink. "They need a timetable."

Quiet applause interrupts, and the quartet members bow, smile, and make their way down the gazebo's steps to four chairs set apart from the rest. Reverend Wilkins, an imposing blimp of a man in a gray suit with a white boutonnière, circles the gazebo and mounts it from the opposite side. He smiles, beckons, and at last Phil and I are moving, down the walk, up the gazebo steps. The Reverend shakes hands with Phil and me, says a few calming words that escape me now, prompts me to face the crowd.

There she is. Janet has appeared out of nowhere, an angel smiling from within a billowed cloud of antebellum white. Our quartet begins the Wagner processional. She and her coterie walk the sinuous path, float up the gazebo steps. Standing before me, she's so effervescent. One might interpret her mood as silly, but that's not so. She's expressive, that's all, like Phil. And happy. She's happy. So am I.

A red curl has strayed across her forehead, bouncing on a passing breeze. For some reason, I can't settle for anything less than perfection today, so I step forward, touch the curl back into place. She breathes out, a little apprehensive, then amused. She glances to Phil. They laugh, ever so softly.

She whispers something and takes my hand. I nod without hearing, my attention lost in the depths of those blue eyes.

"That's so beautiful," Aunt Carol sobs from the crowd, stirring a titter of laughter.

"So tender," someone else adds.

Mom. I have to see her reaction. Ever the cigar store Indian, she sits erect, back ramrod straight, impassive.

Reverend Wilkins clears his throat, smiles at the crowd. He begins: "Those of you who know Janet and John as well as I realize this marriage will endure."

He continues with his remarks, my attention drifting to a globe of birds hidden in the branches beyond. They're excited, too, but then their chirps grow dim, far away. The trees thin, no longer oaks, but pines. We're almost above them, Janet and I, hand in hand on a bare hillock near our home, overlooking Lake Lanier. This is our special place, our point of release from my work, and hers.

Every day after her classes at Emory – she's majoring in journalism – she settles into the den with a legal pad. While I'm laboring over that first novel in the attic, she calls agents and editors, a few literary journals and commercial magazines, soliciting interest in my work. Her voice is like music to me, a comfort, lost as I am in the wilds of yet-untamed imagination. When I can't hear her singsong, the cheery laughter, her sandals clacking across the den's wooden floor, I have to stop. Then, locating her, I exhale relief and return to work.

But this hillock is our respite, our place of recreation and, hopefully, celebration. Janet spreads a red-and-white checkered tablecloth just past the crest so we can watch sailboats on the lake. I pull a bottle of cheap chardonnay from an ice bucket and undo the cork. We picnic on sandwiches, pickles and chips from a wicker basket, drinking wine straight from the bottle. A delicious vice, something I'm sure Hemingway would have enjoyed were he seventy years younger and writing in the urban South.

Our lunch is light, almost without substance, and the wine goes straight to my head. "Any takers today?" tumbles from somewhere inside me.

The wind luffs Janet's hair, the way it's abusing a catamaran's blue and white sail on the lake. She smiles, shrugs, tugs her attention away from the lake's breezy waters.

"Everyone knows your name now, John. Just a matter of the right piece in the right hands."

Then the stack of unpaid bills on her desk grows in my mind's eye, looms like a storm. "I'm not making any money," I say. "You're earning the living and doing half my work."

She crawls to me, sits on her heels, and cups my concerned pout in both hands. "An investment," she says. She kisses me.

Her coy encouragement doesn't alleviate my sense of impending doom. "You're making us sound like a business arrangement. With me receiving all the benefits."

"Well, yes, it is a business arrangement." She laughs. "And a lot more."

This anxiety of mine surfaces regularly, more virulent than the constant self-doubt that's always been characteristic of creative types. But it's never hit me this forcefully before. Something's wrong. I can't describe it yet, but it's there, lurking, just beyond the senses. I've lost my moorings, Janet my only connection. Take her in your arms, John, kiss her, don't let her go.

After a long kiss, she pushes away, ever so gently, and eyes me. "What is it, baby? What's wrong?"

"I don't know. Getting edgy about doing all this work and not getting paid for it, I guess."

She toys with the top button of my polo shirt, thinking. Then she lifts her face to mine and laughs, the teasing, little girl laugh that erases all care. "You writers, you have to strike this existential pose, don't you?"

There. The laughter is infectious, grounding me. Really grounding me. She buries her face in my billowing shirt. We laugh together.

"Then we should make existential love," I blurt, what I've been wanting all morning.

She looks up, moppet-eyed, not sure whether I'm serious or returning the tease. "You don't mean here." She twists a knot in the front of her tee shirt with one hand, fingers of the other as wriggly as a can of worms.

"Here." I point to the tablecloth. "It already has mustard stains on it."

She exhales pertly, eyes me with glee. Always up for mischief, this girl. "Okay," she says, drawing the word out. "But how do we go about –"

Now it's my turn to laugh. "We take off our clothes, for starters."

At first she tries to hide her essentials behind a hand, a turned back, a crossed leg. Then something takes her. She stands. She shouts into the breeze and turns a full circle, falls into my arms. We lose ourselves in one another.

Time fast-forwards. The sun has descended a hand or two, the lake a glare, soft breezes rising from it. We're still naked, stretched out on our sides facing one another, taking turns at the wine. The day's grown warm, and we're flushed with sweat. We must be gleaming like a pair of mirrors. Something about the idea strikes me as significant. I close my eyes, try to picture it.

"John!"

She points, the other arm over her breasts. Then the noise – an approaching helicopter. It hovers, turns in a tight circle and edges away, backward, nose down. The pilot and another man are smiling. We wave and laugh. The chopper dips, then hurries past the cliffs and disappears into the sun. Its noise goes silent, replaced by the hollow calls of a pair of hawks riding updrafts, their back-and-forth resembling faint laughter.

A naughty, clandestine giggle and inaudible words reach me. "…in the morning. You, too."

Janet clicks off the phone, tiptoes to the bed, sets it on its stand. My breathing is still a deep, regular, raspy growl.

"John!" Her lips are close enough for me to feel her breath on my ear. My eyes open a crack. She smiles, but worry has taken the twinkle from those blue eyes. "Get dressed, John. I just heard the car drive up." She scrambles around the bed and toward the door.

I stand, leg up my trousers, and call out, "Who was on the phone?"

She stops, wheels, mouth pursed. She re-enters the bedroom. Her brow wrinkles, eyes narrowed.

"Don't ask," Ezra advises, his voice now thickened by a German accent.

"…her that," Michael adds, giving up an elfin giggle.

Janet's frown dissolves, replaced by a slowly forming stare, her head tilting to one side. She forces a smile. "You weren't asleep?" Despite the matter-of-fact tone she affects, there's an undercurrent of alarm.

"Sort of," I try to explain as I button my shirt, squirm into my shoes. "I was dreaming, in and out."

Ezra's and Michael's hoots become a deafening cacophony, and I try to swat them away, to no avail.

"Are you all right?" Her expression shifts to concern.

"Figments." With this forthright admission, my two alter egos fall silent.

"Did you take your medicine?"

A nod. "And an extra, after Mom and Ted came."

The front door's opening. Janet pulls me from the bedroom and toward the stairs, leads the way down. One, two, three…

Ted waltzes in, clearly excited, carrying two shopping bags. He's now dressed in slacks and a buttoned shirt. Strange. He hates that sort of clothing. He bounces into the den. Huh. He never acts like that. Mom follows, holding another, larger shopping bag, from an upscale department store at the Mall of Georgia.

Night has completed its intrusion, adding definition to the den's subtle hues. Janet begins to draw the shades. For some reason, she leaves one bare – the one facing the lake. Somewhere in the distance, a great horned owl announces its presence, probably to some cowering prey.

They return to their original seats, Janet and Ted on the couch, Mom in the caned chair. I sag once more into the rocker. The TV's still on, muted. After a few clicks, a famous former Marine officer begins one of his weekly war stories.

"Can I show them, Grandma?" Ted asks. He's now radiating effervescence, a rarity these days, to say the least. But there's no way this can survive Mom's leveling gaze. He sniffs, mimics her rigid posture, becomes a virtual statue.

Her glance sweeps by me, to Janet. "I only intended to buy Ted a few things to make him more presentable at school, but from what he told me, he's terribly lacking."

"Grandma," Ted whines, acting and looking half his age. Odd.

She sighs in a breath, draws her mouth into a severe line with the exhale. "All right."

He opens one bag, then the other, displays polo shirts, slacks, underwear, socks, then a pair of ties and a carefully folded blue blazer. He lunges for Mom's bag and proudly produces a pair of expensive sneakers and two pairs of loafers, one brown, the other black.

Janet's been watching the unveiling, arms folded, chin thrust out and askew. When Ted got to the ties and blazer, her eyes narrowed and she threw me a razor-sharp glance. She now wriggles to the front of her couch cushion and leans forward. "I'm not sure why all this is necessary," she says in a demanding voice. She twists to face Ted. "Was this your idea, all these things? You have a closet full of clothes."

His animation dissipates completely, embryonic Adam's apple bobbing.

Janet squints at Mom, fingers of both hands alternating between wriggles and air-pounding, clenched-white fists. "Then this was your idea." She starts in a low, husky voice, but it quickly amplifies to yelling. "You know we can't afford things like this. You're trying to make us look bad to Ted. You're trying to buy him away from us."

A huff escapes Mom, presaging a deep, intent frown. "I hardly think I'm the one to make you look bad."

Janet sways, twists, trying to restrain more venom. Fat chance. She looks to me, as if to say, Well, John? Why don't you stop this? When I don't, she grinds her teeth. Her squint finds Mom once more. "You are such a bitch."

Mom's eyes narrow. "If I were you, Janet, I'd watch what I say around Ted. Children his age gain or lose respect for their elders by the examples they set."

Janet rises to a crouch, fists at her chest, ready to leap into combat. "You'd do what?" she shrieks.

"Sit down." Mom's growled words carry all the authority of a drill sergeant.

"Catfight," shrills Carly.

"Behave, sister," says Lana. "You want to have things your way? Then learn from the master. Mistress, I mean."

I shouldn't be watching passively, no matter how enthralling. It's time to interfere. My mouth sags open, presaging words.

Janet notices, of course. "Don't, John," she snaps. "It's time your mother and I had this out."

Mom nods. She's trying to conceal a gleam. Oh, no, I see what's happening. She's setting Janet up. What's she going to say?

"But setting a good example apparently isn't one of your talents, Janet," Mom replies in her most casual manner.

Janet knows her, but not like I do. Mom's playing the game a half-dozen moves ahead. I can tell she already smells victory.

"I told you both," Mom goes on, "Ted's returning to Augusta with me."

Janet has involuntarily obeyed Mom's dictum to sit, but now she's wriggling toward that crouch again.

Carly shrieks with glee. "Claw the old goat's face, bitch," she calls out.

Janet tenses, as if she's heard the taunt.

Mom's jaw tightens. So resolute. "When we return, I'm enrolling him in Augusta Christian School. They require a tie and blazer." She nods toward the pile of clothes at Ted's feet. "It's convenient, and it's a fine school. Not a cesspool, like the public ones."

Janet begins stamping a foot. "No! Ted's our son. You don't have a right to even talk this way."

"I have every right. Ted's father is ill. He belongs in a hospital, not trying to continue the illusion that he's a writer."

"I'm writing," I complain. "Fifteen pages today."

"And tomorrow?" Her eyes bore into me, as if I'm a child interfering in an adult discussion.

Unable to withstand this withering glare, my head falls forward. "I don't know."

"You'll never know, Johnny, not anymore. It's over for you. The sooner you come to grips with that, the sooner you'll realize you need better help than you're getting."

Janet's been trying to interject something, but the sobs she keeps swallowing won't let anything out. This isn't a battle, it's a rout. Finally, she regains a semblance of composure. "Even if John eventually needs more medical help, I'll still be here." Her words are determined, metronomic in their cadence. "It'd be harder to manage things, but I would do what John needs. I can easily see Ted through school."

Mom's chiseled features have relaxed. She doesn't need that austere focus now; her footing's safe, victory all but assured. "That might be true, if you could withstand a competency hearing."

"What?" Janet blanches. "What do you mean?"

Mom glances my way, then to Ted, who has lunged from the couch. He's sitting on his heels on the rug, hands on thighs, as if a muezzin has called him to prayer.

The buzzing, abrupt as a door slam – my ears are ringing with it, vision clouded. When this clears, Ted's suddenly back in jeans and blue polo shirt, on his knees between Mom and Janet. How odd. And where did they put the packages, the new clothing of Ted's?

"I'm back," he declares.

Of course he is. And he's afraid of where this is heading. He's breathing in gasps, sweating, as if he's been running. I think he wants to say something. What's he saying? Does he really want to talk now?

Mom stops him with a loud throat clearing and a halting hand. She glares at Janet. "Let's just say there's a moral standard you wouldn't be able to meet."

Ted gapes, panic flooding him. He looks to the front door, probably planning another escape. He's mumbling again, guilt-faced, about someone who called, might drop by. See? He too can't deal with reality when it gets this intense.

Janet's mouth hangs open, too, her eyes mirroring Ted's panic for a second. She slumps into the couch. She's trying to disappear. Her furtive glance my way says, "I'm sorry." But for what?

"Do I have to spell it out, Janet? Do you really want that? Here in front of Johnny and Ted?"

What are they talking about? What's Janet done that's so awful? She goes to work, makes the living for us. She pays the bills and makes sure Ted's seen to.

Mom's carefully crafted smile belies her rapacious eyes. "Well, Janet?"

"Do something, big guy," says Carly. "You have to do something."

But what can I possibly do at this point? You don't step between these two unless you want to get caught in a crossfire.

"Leave him alone, sister," says Lana. "Let me think."

"Look," says Carly, "if you can fix this with John, you can have him. I won't interfere anymore."

"I'm thinking," says Lana. Then resolve floods her. "Okay, got it." There's a whooshing sound.

Janet, as if struck by a thunderbolt, straightens, leans toward Mom. The hurt and panic are gone. She sneers. "The better question is whether *you* want to get into this." She nods in my direction, eyes never leaving Mom. "John's my Exhibit A. You try to ruin our marriage, I'll make sure he tells a judge about the childhood you ruined."

They jabber back and forth, voices rising. Verbal punches are being thrown left and right, and they're all drawing metaphorical blood. The whole thing starts making me sick, but what can I do? The buzzing's rising to siren pitch. Do something, John, anything.

"No, don't!" My voice – I'm yelling. Didn't realize they had me that upset. "Please."

Janet seems duly chastised, but Mom, she's mad, really mad. Haven't seen her face this red and bloated since I was Ted's age. They've stopped their squabble, though, so the stage is mine. Must say more, but what? Mouth, so dry.

"Ted, I realize you're caught up in all this," I declare in a halting voice as I make a few wild, inclusive hand gestures. Now I'm turning back and forth between Janet and Mom, mostly in what will surely be a futile attempt to have them see reason. "Are you trying to help? Or do you just want a fight, see who wins? Because if you do, well…"

Not particularly eloquent, but they're both staring, and a bit more respectfully. I must have made my point.

"Oh my," Lana exclaims, her voice filled with awe as she gives her bosoms a squeeze.

"I take it back," says Carly. "I want him. Right now. Damn, he's hot."

Good grief. How do they do it, these figments? My slacks, they're about to burst, even after the session Janet and I just had. I'm exploding. Wriggle around, John, don't let them see it.

Janet nods. "You're right, John. You're right." Her lower lip quivers, a faint moan escapes, and her eyes swell and glisten. She turns, pushes herself from the couch to the floor. She reaches for Ted.

Ted recoils. Suddenly, they're both crying, Janet's arms around him. This is great. This is what I wanted, Ted and Janet united, on the same emotional page.

But Mom. She's really, really agitated. She twists in her chair, hisses out a sigh. Suddenly she straightens, as if impaled by the same lightning bolt that hit Janet. She turns. "Johnny, do you know what she's done to you? Do you know what your wife is doing?"

"No!" Ted screams. He stares at me, unbelieving, frightened, then looks away.

Janet's bleary eyes find Mom, the old lady's fierce stare growing in intensity. Janet's sobs come in fits.

"She's involved with someone else," Mom says. "Someone she works with." She pivots in her chair to face Ted. "Ted, darling, what did you say his name was?"

He bursts into another fit of bawling.

"You bitch!" Janet yells above Ted's wails.

Mom extends an arm, palm upward, gives me a smug look. "Do you see, Johnny? Do you see what's going on around you? Are you sane enough to comprehend what's transpired?"

"All right!" yells Janet. "I'll tell him!"

"No," says Mom, "I want Ted to tell his father why he's left. He's disgusted with you, Janet, with the way you've handled your responsibilities. There's more to it than inattention to you, Johnny. Tell him, Ted, tell your father what you told me."

I have to calm him somehow. "All right then, what is it, son? Tell me."

Ted's contorted face flushes with confusion.

God, was I ever that disturbed? Did I ever let things between Mom and Dad get to me like this? The truth is, I can't remember. I remember the low points, Mom badgering Dad for days on end. His yelling at her, then disappearing into the basement, where he'd stay for days. Mom, relentless, calculating, unfeeling, badgering him through the basement door. I don't remember. Just don't remember how those days were for me. It had to have been bad, though.

Is that what Dr. Blucher's been driving at, the questions he continually slips into our conversations about Mom, Dad, me? Is that why I'm so taken with the earlier Persian Gulf War, with the one about to begin? Maybe they remind me of those days of internecine warfare at home. But no matter how bad a domestic situation becomes for a child, a sense of security still hovers, like a warm memory. It's home, it's family. It's real. These Middle East wars, maybe they do seem like those childhood years, but this time it's a conflict I can watch, on TV, as a non-combatant. No, I can't ever be safe from conflict, not where Ted's concerned.

He climbs awkwardly to his feet, stumbles to me. His head's hanging, one hand wringing the other against his chest, the picture of contrition. He mumbles into his shirt, something he really doesn't want me to hear. Something about Janet. At least that's what I think he's saying. He ends with some inaudible addendum.

My eyelids begin to shimmy. It's hard to make out faces, and my eyes are burning. So is my throat. I'm parched.

"Janet is an editor for the Gainesville Times-Herald," Mom says. Now her voice has gone pubescent, sort of like Ted's. "And she works for the editor-in-chief. His name is Evan Barnicke. Janet's been having sex with him. Do you know what that means? Do you understand what having sex means?"

"Yes! I know!" I have to lower the volume, try to be calm. "I know," I repeat, calmer now. Does she think I'm an idiot, or maybe brain-dead? I'm not. I see, hear figments, that's all. That's all? That's enough.

"Good," she says, almost gooey with satisfaction. "Then you know she can't be trusted with your welfare, or Ted's."

"We had sex," I blurt, not sure why it's so important to add this. "While you were gone."

"Stop it!" Ted moans. He lurches away, stumbles toward Mom. You'd think a teenaged boy wouldn't be so upset at talk of parental sex.

Mom holds out her arms. "That's it, Ted, come to Grandma." For a long while, he doesn't move. Then he approaches her, stops just out of reach, turns to me. She hurls a glare toward Janet, who is sitting on her heels, hands at chest level, each its usual kettle of snakes, eyes glowing red with upset. Or is it shame? Not sure, really, but she's beaten, defeated, her secret out. That's what Mom can do to you if you get in her way.

I know Evan, he's a nice guy. Maybe he and Janet just talk. Janet probably needs someone to talk to. I can't fill that bill, or hardly any other, so maybe she bends his ear over lunch.

Mom's going theatrical now, pretending she's in anguish over this. "The mother of some boy Ted knows, divorced, isn't she, Ted? She drives the boy to school every day, then out to lunch. They've seen Janet having lunch with this person, this editor-in-chief, this supervisor of hers, and he's seen them holding hands. Last week, Ted's friend saw them kissing in a car at a filling station."

Ted, who's been staring at me, lowers his trembling chin to his shirt.

Mom spreads her hands, palms up. She lifts her eyebrows, mouth taut, as if saying, "There, you see?" She turns to glare at Janet, who has returned to the couch. "Do you have anything to say for yourself, young lady?"

Janet returns the look, in spades. "Go to hell."

Mom partially stifles a mean laugh. "I hardly think I'm the one to worry about that."

Time to break this up. But for some reason, I'm making gurgling noises, can't speak.

Ted's nearby. He doubles his fists, clenches and unclenches. "I said stop it!" he shouts again, crimson rising in him.

Janet bites her lip, fights back tears. She hugs her shoulders, nods in Ted's direction, squares up to Mom. "And you think you'd be a fit parent for Ted? How much more of this are you willing to put him through?"

There! Mom's lip trembles. So she's fallible after all. Who would have thought she wouldn't have anticipated this sort of counterattack from Janet?

"Janet," I begin, not knowing what to feel, much less what to say. So I simply shrug.

Janet pats the couch cushion next to her and waggles her finger, beckoning. Who can resist that? I rise, approach, sit. She leans into me, my shirt swallowing her.

"I'm so sorry, John."

After a handful of sobs she leans away, takes a deep breath and scoots into a corner pillow, sitting cross-legged. That beautiful, translucent face, still twisted and red. The deep blue eyes hidden behind a sheen of the same red hue. She tugs at a red curl hanging over her left ear. So vulnerable. But we need to talk about Evan.

"You love me?" That's all I know to whisper, really, the only thing that matters. If she loves him, then she doesn't love me. If she doesn't love me, what will I do? How will I fight these figments, this jumbled mess in my head?

"I don't know," she whispers in reply. "I don't know." And Ted's mirroring her ambivalence.

I want to go deeper into this, to distil my own emotions into one crystalline statement. But it's like trying to manage blood spurting from a severed artery.

She bawls, head in hands, and then forces the crying to a halt. "This has been so hard, John. I haven't had anyone to talk to since you've been sick." She sniffs. "I wanted to be strong, to help, you know?"

"You can never give in," Mom interrupts. "You can't allow yourself the luxury of insecurity and confusion. You simply have to move him forward. With you."

"No, that's what you do," Janet counters. "And see what it got you? A husband who committed suicide and a schizophrenic son."

Before Mom can reply, Janet turns to me again. "I never know what you're thinking, John. I never know how to help you, how to comfort you."

Before replying, I glance to Ted, who stands tense with anguish a few steps away. "I'm okay," I say, nodding. After all, I know a figment when I see one. Oh, I'd rather not have them around. They keep me from sleeping deeply, especially Lana. But what Mom says is true: it's a question of will. You overcome your obstacles and keep going.

Janet's look tells me she's not buying into this. "No, John, you're not okay. You have a mental disease, and it's getting worse. You can't work. You're losing touch with reality. Your social skills are going. And your sense of cleanliness. You're deteriorating right before my eyes, and I don't know what to do about it."

By now I'm expecting Mom to jump in, to marginalize Janet again, to tell me she, Mom, has all the answers. Instead, she's staring at Janet, the steel in those slate-blue eyes somehow softened, replaced by, what? Hurt? Do I sense sympathy here? Does what she's hearing from Janet strike some sort of chord?

"The medicine isn't working for you," Janet goes on. "We need to talk to Dr. Blucher about that. I'm going with you Wednesday. We'll ask."

The medication I'm taking is the least of my concerns. It's a palliative, that's all, something to calm me, cause me not to worry about the figments, about my condition. Janet and Dr. Blucher, they decide these things without my approval. To hell with them and their medicine. This affair, lost love, that's my concern. I picture Evan kissing Janet.

Janet wipes away a new spate of tears and nods, knowing full well what's on my mind. "Yes, I did that, John. I let him romance me. I wanted to be normal again, I —"

"You're normal. I'm the one that's not."

She shakes her head. "You're not an island, John. Your disease doesn't stop with you. It affects everyone you touch. Look what it's done to Ted. And me. It's forced me away."

Despite the melodramatic tone, I get her point. Okay, I've been too self-absorbed, but the disease does that, or so Dr. Blucher tells me. Is she going to leave me? Has Evan already replaced me? I have to know.

"You're going to leave me?"

She moans, sounding as distressed and defeated as I often feel.

Maybe she's right, maybe a disease like mine finds ways to skirt the barriers loved ones invariably erect in their effort to remain individuals. Maybe the sickness seeps invisibly into everyone about you. Still, there's one question I have to clarify. It's the big one, the only one left.

"You don't love me?"

This time her tears flow unimpeded. After she's stanched them, she scoots near, falls into me, her slender arms taking a barely tangible hold.

Mom's shuffling her feet – a most uncharacteristic tic, and looking to the flooring knot that Michael calls home.

Ted. Something's up with him. He's stone-faced, rigid, as if he can't move from the spot he's standing on, to Mom's right. Something's not right, and already I'm afraid of what I'm seeing in him.

But Janet. She's tacitly answered my question. She does love me.

FIVE

"I'm going to my room," Ted announces. Flustered and red-faced, he dashes to the stairs and bounds up them. His door slams.

Janet scoots away, still bleary-eyed. "How could you do this to us?" she demands of Mom.

"How could *you?*" Mom challenges. "You want me to be the problem, Janet. Why is that?"

I don't want to face another one of their rounds, so I slip onto the rocker again, nudge the TV's sound up, just enough to hear. On CNN, a reporter stands atop a flat-roofed building and talks of the mood on the Baghdad streets. Lightning-like flashes, and then dull thumps shake the building. The aerial bombardment that's been growing for days is reaching a crescendo. Fires are everywhere.

The reporter dives, flattens himself against the roof's surface, glances over his shoulder toward the building's edge. For a moment he goes quiet, the camera bobbing before him as if at the mercy of a storm ravaged sea. Beyond, and sounding far away, the rattle of small arms fire. Talking animatedly and acting as tough he relishes all this, the reporter raises a finger six inches from his microphone, tells us a round, probably from a Kalashnikov, has just missed him and the photographer.

Michael pulls my attention away. No, it's not Michael. It's a composite, a blending of Mom and Janet's voices, arguing. No, it's Michael, for real this time.

"We don't have to stay here, you know," he says. "We can go to the lake."

I tell him it's dark, but I don't think I'm talking aloud. It's more than thought, though, some form of communication he and I must have practiced to perfection. But where is he?

Then that silly laugh of his. "The window," he says, "that's your gateway to freedom."

Sure enough, his odd little body is perched on the windowsill, legs dangling. Such a strange fellow. He turns, hunkers, and peers into the dark, toward the lake. "It's such a nice night out," he says. "C'mon."

"No!"

Uh oh. I spoke out loud that time, shouted, in fact. Mom and Janet's conversation stops short. They stare at me, then exchange looks.

"It's the war," Mom says. "He shouldn't be watching such things. It'll make his state worse."

"It's all right," Janet tries to explain. "He's working on an essay for a magazine. It's research."

I shake my head and point toward the window. Now why did I do that? I certainly don't want them to know about Michael. So I jerk my hand back and start fumbling with the remote. It falls to my lap, then the floor.

"He's hallucinating," Mom states flatly. "Dropping the remote? That was a cover-up."

Janet's perplexed. "Cover-up?"

"Of course. I'm surprised you haven't learned to read these things by now." Mom goes on, claiming that I don't want to share my hallucinatory experiences, that it would make me seem hopelessly deranged if I did. She's been reading about the psychology of schizophrenia, and despite seeing me only rarely, she claims an ability to interpret my most insignificant gestures. Well, why not? She can read my mind, can't she?

But they shouldn't waste such scrutiny on me. Ted. What about Ted? Time to rise, stir around a bit, shake things up. It chases away the figments. It gets the blood flowing, makes me feel normal. "Ted," I begin, retrieving the remote and placing it on the end table as I stand. He's the issue here, not me. "What's he doing?"

Janet gives me an odd squint. "He went to his room. You saw him stomp up the stairs. He was very upset."

"I doubt John noticed," Mom says. "When they get caught up in hallucinations, they don't notice anything else."

"They?" Janet's shriek returns. "It's not as though John's not aware. Stop talking about him as if he weren't here."

Mom's ire is back full force, too. She smirks, and then her lips draw to a sneer. These two, they seem to have been somewhat in accord for a moment, but now they're going to have at one another again. How quickly harmony can turn to conflict. Mom gives Janet a sour look, turns my way, cocks a critical eyebrow. Or is she looking for an ally? Does she really expect me to take her side against Janet?

"Johnny," Mom asks, "why were you asking about Ted?"

She waits for my answer, but I'm not finding one. Time to sit again. She leans toward me, rubs her neck. It's her arthritis, I think, or maybe that injury she incurred recently, a fender-bender, I think. "You do realize he went to his room, don't you?"

"Yes."

"Then what's the problem?"

My mouth, it's always dry when I'm on the hot seat like this. Wish I could find a glass of water. Have to go to the kitchen. No, too far, too much trouble. Go ahead, John, answer her question, show her you're not catatonic.

"Don't fight about Ted." That's what's on my mind. "Help him. He needs help."

Mom faces Janet once more, gives a smug, satisfied sigh. She thinks I have no understanding of what they've been saying, that they've been talking about Ted instead of about me.

Janet parses the implications of this and then says, "Well, Ted's not going to Augusta, and that's final."

Mom ignores her, rolls her shoulders forward once, twice, then back. It's the neck pain. Or maybe she's biding time, deliberating.

"Perhaps in a way you're right, Janet," she says with a nod.

What? She's saying we're right about something? When has anyone ever been right but her? What's she up to? Uh oh. She's turning those laser eyes on me. Look away, John. Please, don't look at me like that!

"As I think about it," Mom goes on, "Johnny is the larger issue. If it weren't for his infirmity, your marriage would be on solid ground. And that would allow my grandson a little growing space." She smiles, one of those grim, forced smiles she occasionally fashions, always a prelude to something she wants, something she's sure she'll get.

One loud moan escapes Janet before she can collect herself. "I know." Her reply comes out weak, as if agreeing with Mom sticks in her throat. Still, she senses Mom's up to something. She looks to me, beseechingly, unsure, afraid.

Sorry, Janet. I know the old lady so well, but how do I communicate what I feel, what I know? Mom's changing tactics, she's going to divide and conquer. Now that she's exposed Janet's affair, she's going to play on her guilt. She's going to surrender me to Janet in order to get Ted. No surprise there. She gave up on me years ago, when I married Janet. Janet's strong-willed, though hardly a match for Mom, and the old lady has always despised that in her.

Mom turns her eyes to the floor, but she isn't able to hide their triumphant gleam. Face lifted to me once more, the eyes are clear, intense.

"Johnny, I was just thinking. You do remember Aunt Billie, don't you?"

Aunt Billie. Haven't heard that name in years. Not since Mom decreed her name wasn't to be spoken in our family again. Yes, nodding. Sure, I remember Aunt Billie. Poor Aunt Billie.

"Aunt Billie?" Janet's flummoxed. "I've never heard that name." She looks to me, as if to ask why I've never mentioned her.

I can't tell the story, so what am I to do? Look away, that's all. Just look away. It's not a story I dare get into.

"She died in her twenties," Mom says. Well. She's going to reopen this, after all these years. She goes on. "Mother was the oldest of eight children, Billie the youngest. Billie was my senior by ten years."

"She died?" Janet asks. "How?"

"She was a nurse. Bright, a good student. Very popular. Creative. She painted. Johnny, you remember those oil canvases of hers I kept, don't you?"

Why is she going to air this? I mean, what's the point? What does Aunt Billie have to do with Ted, or me?

"Johnny!"

I get it. She's challenging me. Daring me. She's going to say I'm like Aunt Billie. Do I have to take this? I have to fight back. Have to try. Don't want to end up like Billie. Yes, nodding, I remember those awful, disturbed paintings.

"Good," she says, softly.

Those dark paintings, filled with such melancholy. They've always reminded me of Edvard Munch's stuff, with the looming trees and brooding houses, the vacant, somber people. You always hope such works don't represent the artist's feelings or emotional makeup. But with Aunt Billie, we had to assume they did.

Bits of her handed-down history begin to reveal themselves now, like snippets of bad dreams. Two years after completing nursing school, Billie began having problems, started shutting herself off from her friends. At least that's what Mom and Aunt Carol used to say, before Mom forbade us to speak of her.

Aunt Billie didn't perform well in the operating room, she forgot the procedures, the protocol. The surgical instruments began to confuse her. So one morning, Georgia Baptist Hospital's head surgeon stopped by Grandpa's office to chat about her. Or, rather, the quality of her work. Grandpa promised he'd take her aside and talk.

That night after dinner, so the story goes, he asked Billie, who was living with Grandma and Grandpa at the time, to his den. They walked in silence through the white brick, two-story house's dimly lit hallway to the front-most room. From here the story is strictly conjecture – mine. But Grandpa, a tall, handsome, black-haired railroad executive, probably flicked on the overhead chandelier and hung his suit coat on a rack just inside the door. Unbuttoned his vest and loosened his tie, opened a carved hickory humidor set on the desk's front corner, and selected a cigar. After precisely correcting the humidor's position on the desk, he drew his smoke to coals and settled into his high-backed desk chair.

Aunt Billie edged onto the front of a similar, smaller chair before the desk. Her delicate hands moved from her lap to a clench at the throat, then back, the white of her bare forearms luminous against the chair's black leather. She blanched at Grandpa's easy, evaluating look. Her eyes frantically swept the room.

After a minute or so of silence, Grandpa rose and took a bottle of whiskey from a glass-doored cabinet on an adjacent wall.

"Would you like one, Billie?"

"What? Oh. I mean, no, thank you, Robert. It-it's Thursday, and I have work tomorrow."

"Of course." He poured. Raising his glass to the light, he swirled the brown fluid, sipped, gave a satisfied sigh, and took his seat. "How has work been?"

"Fine. That is, I, well, I-I'm still learning the protocol. It's very complicated, you see, and –"

"Doctor Hunt came by this morning." He again sipped the whiskey and wriggled comfortably into his chair.

"He did? But why? I-no one said anything at work. I'm doing fine. I'm sure I am." She stopped suddenly, clutched at the row of decorative buttons over her breast. "What did he want?"

"He had some concerns regarding your performance in the operating room. I promised him I'd talk with you about it."

"I dropped the retractors," she said, voice rising to a tense pitch. "He wanted a scalpel, but I handed him something –"

"A sponge."

She slumped. "Really?"

"Doctor Hunt wouldn't have the story wrong. Is that what happened?"

"Well, I suppose so."

"You're not sure?"

Head in hands now, she began to cry. "No."

"Why, Billie?"

She began writhing, her shoes' leather soles scratching back and forth on the wooden floor. "I don't know."

Grandpa's brow drew into a frown, his mouth pursed. He set down his glass and leaned forward. "Is it that you don't remember?"

"I don't know!" She scrambled to her feet, flung the door open, and raced out, up the stairs to her room, her loud wails reaching Grandma in the kitchen.

Grandma went to comfort her, but Billie wouldn't unlock her door. Two hours later, after the wails had ended, Grandma unlocked the door and slipped into the darkened room. Billie lay curled in a fetal position, fully clothed and sound asleep.

Five days later, the hospital let her go.

The following week, Billie ran away.

I've been looking to the window, and now realize Mom and Janet are staring. But why? Is someone talking to me? Or are they trying to measure my reaction to Mom's mentioning Billie? Probably just a solemn interlude, by the looks of it. I try to react appropriately, to seem wistful, but I can't. I'm nervous. Nervous as hell.

It's apparent that Mom's been telling a parallel version of the story, and waiting for me to acknowledge it. But I sense something else coming, something she thinks will resolve my situation. I give her the look she expects, indicating recognition of the story and agreement with her telling. She continues. This time I'm all ears.

"A few days later, Billie ran away. Of course, the family was in an uproar over it. We had cousins and aunts and uncles looking for her, calling her oldest friends, her associates at the hospital, even Doctor Hunt.

"It took two days, but we found her filthy, walking the streets of Atlanta's West Side. Papa decided she had to be under a doctor's care. Not a GP, mind you, another kind of doctor, one more able to help her. She made such a fuss about it."

Mom turns a fabricated smile my way. "You remember how emotional she could be, don't you, Johnny?"

A nod. Who wouldn't be emotional in such a predicament? Family carting you off to a doctor against your will, prying into your innermost feelings. I'm about to ask Mom why they didn't sit with her, get her to open up about whatever was troubling her. Instead, she goes on.

"So Mama and Papa took her to this doctor. They were gone a long while, almost all day. When they brought Billie home, Papa took me aside, told me she was sick. A special kind of sickness, one conventional medicines couldn't affect. He told us the doctor wanted the family to move Billie to a sanitarium.

"At the time, I thought a sanitarium was an awful place, and so did everyone else. Papa refused to institutionalize her. We would hire a nurse, keep her home, so she could remain in familiar surroundings. He wanted her to have the support of family." Again, the unreal smile, this time turned in Janet's direction. "He believed the support of those closest could mean the difference between deterioration and salvation. But it didn't work out that way. At home, we simply couldn't give Billie the help she needed."

Outside, a dove moans. The flooring knot at Mom's feet moves, and suddenly Michael's standing between her knees, looking around, scratching his round tummy. Then he steps away. He waves for me to follow, takes five long strides, leaps, and soars through the window, toward the lake.

I have to blink, this athletic feat of Michael's unbelievable. Dr. Blucher tells me these figments usually act in a typically human manner, that their believability is what makes them so dangerous to my well-being. But by what physics could Michael have done that? Rubbing my eyes doesn't help make his feat any more realistic, and neither does what's going on now at the window.

Vince leans on the sill, this time in a smoking jacket, silk shirt, and gray ascot. He crosses one Gucci over the other, taps the floor with the toe – sans sound. And he too nods toward the darkness leading to the lake and cliffs. "Hear the hawks, John?" he asks. He turns, bends, and peers into the night. Glancing back, he points a thumb in the lake's direction.

What's this? The hawks are squawking in the distance, as if it's still daytime. "Cree-dom. Cree-dom!"

How strange. Now they're laughing. Uproarious laughter. Fun, that's it. They're having fun. Incredible.

Fun. The lake. It's fun at the lake. I acknowledge Vince's point with a shrug.

He laughs, half skeptical of my admission, half amused at my diffidence.

Mom's rationalizations for committing Billie continue unabated. Stand up, John. You need a break. Make an excuse, slip out, run.

"Then," says Mom, waving me back to the rocker, "after twenty-five years or so, her moment of truth came. Johnny was just starting school. You remember the Chattanooga outing, don't you Johnny?"

At the mention of Chattanooga, Vince ducks his head, shrinks visibly. He's nervous, too. But why?

"Johnny," Mom repeats, "do you remember Chattanooga?"

Of course I remember Chattanooga. How could I not remember that day? My hands go to my face. No! I don't want to! Sorry, too late. It's on me, all around me, like a vision from hell.

Grandma had died, Grandpa rather infirm following a depleting illness of some kind. It was the first cool weekend of October. Mom wanted us to go on an outing, but Dad refused unless Mom obtained a weekend pass for Aunt Billie and took her with us. Dad had gone to the store for milk and bread, and I was the only one to witness the row in Grandpa's den. Mom didn't want Grandpa and Aunt Carol in tow, much less Aunt Billie, but Grandpa held his ground. It was one of the few times I remember Mom losing in a battle of wills. Defeated, and after a moment's consideration, she insisted on driving to Cloudland Canyon, near Chattanooga. So she, Dad, Aunt Carol, Aunt Billie, Grandpa, and I piled into Mom's blue Buick.

Cloudland Canyon is a quiet place with spectacular vistas and ample room for picnicking. Trails, should you want to hike. The day before had brought rain, leaving a dome of blue above. The kind of crisp, cool day when the wind will push the frigid air through you and make you laugh at the shivers.

Mom edged the Buick to a stop before a stubby stone wall at the canyon's edge. Aunt Carol helped Grandpa out. At the car's opposite side, Mom tugged Aunt Billie, who refused to budge. The two began arguing. As I helped Dad take a picnic basket, blankets, and our metal cooler from the trunk, we began to get an earful.

"Billie!" Mom growled in her most threatening manner. "Get out. I mean it. We came here today for you to have a nice time, and that's exactly what you're going to do."

Billie had aged terribly. Her straw-blonde hair had thinned due to her constant, nervous pulling, the remaining strands unkempt and showing a sprinkling of gray. She'd lost weight, a wraith of her former self, and she constantly twisted buttons off her clothes. She looked like a haggard beggar.

A story had come to us from the sanitarium that she had torn her clothes to rags and walked naked down the hallway, singing Cole Porter tunes and performing a few Shirley MacLaine dance steps. An attendant stopped her, wrapped her in a blanket. As she was hustled away, Billie announced she was going to urinate on the attendant. She fought her way out of the blanket, hugged the attendant, and carried out her threat.

But Mom was more than her match the day of the Cloudland Canyon trip. Billie was a head shorter and possibly forty pounds lighter than Mom, who dragged Billie kicking and yelling from the Buick.

"You're a whore, you're a whore," Billie screamed, probably the worst epithet she could muster.

Once outside the car, she tried to claw Mom's face. Mom slapped her. A drool of blood slipped from Billie's mouth and down her chin.

Dad and I exchanged glances, aghast. He suddenly became livid. "Charlene, don't do that, ever again."

Mom glanced past us, to Aunt Carol and Grandpa, who were apparently trying to ignore the fracas. "Shut up, Mitchell," Mom said.

Now nervous, Dad replied in a voice that couldn't conceal its quiver. "She's afraid, can't you see that? She's afraid of the canyon, that she might fall. Please, take her up the hill, away from the edge."

Mom surveyed him down the line of her nose. She sniffed. Then a sneer. "All right."

Billie had quieted and gone limp during Mom and Dad's exchange. Mom suddenly spun her, wrapped her in a vise-like hug, and lifted her off the ground. She lugged Billie that way across the parking lot and into the trees beyond.

Despite the tension, we had a pretty good time after that, at least for a while. Mom had made potato salad and my favorite sandwiches. To supplement, we plucked dill pickles and pickled eggs from huge jars. All except for Aunt Carol and Grandpa, who toyed with their dollops of potato salad. Oh, and we drank from a big jug of iced tea Mom had made. After we had eaten, Grandpa rolled over, face away. Soon he was snoring. Billie began whining, Mom growling threats. Dad and I begged away for a walk along the canyon's precipice.

A few clouds puffed into view high above and drifted southward. On the trail, the silence was so pervasive you could almost touch it. After a while, we decided to clap so we could hear the echoes, and that broke the spell. A breeze swelled and moved in the direction the clouds had taken. Below us in the canyon, a stronger wind hummed.

Later, Dad spotted an eagle in a tall pine a hundred yards ahead and up the rocky ground to our left. While we watched, it lifted from its perch and dove, revealing a nest cradled in the nook between the pine's trunk and a larger branch. A few minutes later, the eagle reappeared with something in its mouth, which it began shredding.

"It has fledglings," said Dad.

And that's when we heard Mom calling, not far behind us on the trail.

"What do you suppose that's all about?" asked Dad.

"Maybe she wants to go home."

Dad smiled at the prospect and cupped a hand over the nape of my neck, gave an affectionate squeeze. "Probably can't wait to get your Aunt Billie back to the sanitarium. Let's sit. She'll find us."

"Johnny!"

Her calls grew stronger.

"Mitchell!"

Dad winked and held a finger to his lips.

"Johnny! Mitchell! I need you. Please!"

Dad frowned. We rose and turned back. In less than two minutes, we heard her stumbling footsteps. Then we saw her, maybe twenty yards down the trail. She was crying.

Dad hurried on ahead, reached for her. She swatted his hand away.

"Where were you?" she cried. "Why didn't you come?"

"What is it, Charlene?" Dad reached to wipe one of her tear-stained cheeks. Again, she batted his hand away.

"Billie's disappeared." Then something remarkable happened. She fell into Dad's arms and sobbed on his shoulder.

"There, there," Dad cooed.

His attempt at comfort must've seemed patronizing, because, still crying, she barked, "Don't!" She pushed away and slapped him, hard.

He staggered back with the surprise assault, almost tripping over me. He rubbed his cheek. "All right, Charlene, tell me what's happened. What this about Billie?"

"It's your fault," Mom screeched. "It's your fault."

Dad's chin quivered a little, and both hands began to shake. "What do you mean? What's my fault?"

"Billie!" Mom screamed. "She wanted to walk with you, but did you care? Did you even ask? No! You and your boy just took off, as if you didn't have a care in the world."

Dad stuttered, then coughed to stanch it. "I – we didn't know."

"Shut up, Mitchell. Just shut up! We have to find her." She spun and lumbered down the trail toward the car.

When Dad and I returned, Aunt Carol and Grandpa were standing under the large pine where we'd picnicked.

"You didn't find her?" Aunt Carol asked in a tremulous voice.

Mom started crying again. Dad tried in his careful, awkward fashion to console her. I shook my head no, we hadn't found Aunt Billie.

"But I don't understand," said Grandpa, nodding toward the trail. "That's the path she took. There's no other place she could've gone."

"What happened?" Dad asked. "Tell me what happened."

"I told you!" Mom screamed. She shoved Dad and began flailing at him with her fists.

Grandpa, weak and no longer able to walk without help, took a step toward Mom. He staggered. Aunt Carol tried unsuccessfully to catch him, and both tumbled to the ground. Mom kept screaming at Dad, kept flailing at him.

"Stop it!" I yelled. I ran to her, began punching her in the back.

She sprawled forward, collapsing Dad's shaky knees. He fell on top of her. She shoved him away, rose to a crouch and swung a flattened hand, the smack reddening Dad's cheek. Tears came to his eyes. I lunged, began punching her in the stomach, the breasts, then the face, with my small fists.

At some point, Dad pulled me away, slipped to his knees and hugged Mom, hard. That ended the brawl.

A minute passed, maybe ten. It was hard to tell in such surreal circumstances. The wild rasp of their combined breathing – Mom's, Dad's, Aunt Carol's and Grandpa's – played against the wind's drone. It took awhile but we collected ourselves, everyone looking to the ground, too embarrassed to speak.

"Come on, Johnny," said Dad as he rose, "let's see if we can find her."

I nodded, eager to escape Mom. Every few feet on the trail, Dad would stop, scramble up the hill, searching. Then he'd ease to the canyon's rim, look over, and shake his head. He'd take my hand firmly in his and we would move on, no words between us.

About halfway between the path's start and where we'd met Mom, a large boulder crowned the rim. It's still covered in graffiti, I imagine, a promontory point for canyon lookers. Dad motioned for me to stay where I was. He scrambled onto the rock and peered into the canyon. He remained motionless for a moment and then wriggled his way back.

Once on the path, he collapsed to a squat, face in his hands. He began to shake.

"She's down there, isn't she?" I said in a hoarse whisper. "Aunt Billie's dead."

He looked up and nodded.

I bawled. Dad reached for me, hugged me to him. We cried together.

Suddenly, I jerked upright. "We have to tell Mom. We have to get Aunt Billie. We have to take her home."

Dad gripped my shoulders, his expression dark. It was a while before he said, "Listen to me, son. Something's wrong here. I need to think this through."

"No!" I wormed away. "We have to get Aunt Billie."

He pulled me to him. I began wailing about Aunt Billie. When I had wound down, he said in an angry, halting voice, "Listen, Johnny. There's something not right about this. I'm going to have to ask some questions."

"I don't know anything," I moaned, afraid he'd thought I'd done something to Aunt Billie.

His voice modulated to a softer, reassuring tone. "I know, son, I know. But promise me something. I'm going to ask your mother a few questions, and it's not going to be the sort of thing a child should hear. So I want you to get in the car, roll the windows up. I don't want you listening to what's being said. Will you do that for me?"

I nodded. He lifted me to my feet, took my hand, and we trudged back down the trail. I kept looking back, crying, hoping to see Aunt Billie.

Then we were back. Without a word, I climbed in the car's back seat and closed the door. One rear window had been rolled down. Dad made circles with a hand, and I cranked it up. He nodded, satisfied. As he turned away, I edged the window back down, maybe a half-inch, enough to prevent the glass from damping the sound of what was going to be said.

Mom edged toward Dad, a hand to her mouth. "Did you –"

He nodded. "We found her. She fell, from quite some height, I believe. I don't think there's any hope."

Aunt Carol began to cry, and Grandpa, too.

"How did it happen that Billie took off walking alone?" Dad asked. "She's deathly afraid of heights."

"I told you," Mom said, stiffening. "She wanted to walk with the two of you. But no, you were so full of yourselves you didn't give her a second thought. So I took off after her."

Even from a distance, I could see the fear in Grandpa's eyes as they flicked between Mom and Dad.

"Charlene," Dad said, his voice now strong, "are you telling me the truth?"

"How dare you!" Mom swung a roundhouse right at Dad. She missed.

He caught her arm and jerked her to her knees. This was an assertive Dad I had never seen before. Mom's mouth fell open, eyes wide.

"Charlene," said Grandpa, pointing at Mom. "She asked Billie if she wanted to take a walk. 'Oh, yes!' Billie told her. She looked toward the path you took, then at the canyon, and she asked Charlene, 'Will you walk me? I'm afraid.' Charlene said she would. 'Go on,' she told Billie, 'go as far as you can. I'll be there in a moment.' Billie looked at her queerly and edged down the trail and out of sight."

Grandpa glanced toward the car, then continued. "I said, 'You shouldn't let her go alone,' but she just smiled and ignored me. I told her I didn't think it was safe. Please, go after her, I said. So she took off, but only after Billie had disappeared up the trail for two, three minutes."

Dad stepped back, bent, and glared at Mom. "Tell me the truth, Charlene."

"No!" Mom screamed. "You think you know, but you don't. I was there, I watched her do it. Before I could stop her, she'd climbed on that big rock you mentioned, and she jumped."

Dad's stare grew luminous. "I never said anything about a big rock, Charlene."

Mom screamed, "I hate her!"

Dad asked, "Why did you do this?"

"I hate her so much," Mom said. "She's so weak and pitiful. She's such a drain —"

Dad stopped her. "You were worried it would take too much of your father's estate to keep her hospitalized. There wouldn't be any left for you."

Mom picked up a handful of gravel and sand and threw it at Dad. "You bastard!"

Some of the fine material found its way into Dad's eyes. He reeled away.

When fingers and tears had flushed the grit away, he turned. "You pushed her, didn't you? You took her along the path to that big rock, and you pushed her over the edge. You murdered your aunt, didn't you?"

"Please," Grandpa pleaded, "don't do this. It won't bring Billie back, so please. Let's just forget it."

Mom stared at Dad for a moment, and then she blinked and bowed her head.

Dad sniffed. "All right. I can't prove anything, so there's no point." He jabbed a finger at her. "But we know, don't we? We'll always know."

We stowed our things. Dad took the wheel, intent on finding a policeman. As we left the park, a ranger truck met us. Dad flagged him down and told him one of our family was dead in the gorge. Dad insisted on taking the ranger there.

When he returned he said to Mom, "We'll have to wait for the police. They need to hear your story. Then we can go."

On the way home, I refused to sit next to Mom. Aunt Carol took my place in the middle of the front seat, Mom and Dad on either side, Grandpa and I in the back. No one spoke during the return trip.

After that, Mom and Dad's feuding escalated, along with Dad's depression. She grew sterner, colder than ever. Dad wouldn't divorce her, but he should have. It would have saved his life.

Now Mom's staring.

"Johnny, what's the matter, son? Aren't you feeling well?"

As if she doesn't know. This is a setup, plain and simple. She's trying to finesse me into something, maybe a sanitarium, like Aunt Billie.

"I'm okay." My hands fall limply to my lap.

Now it's Janet's turn. "Your mom asked you a question, John." She eyes the old goat. "She wants to know what you remember of a Chattanooga outing."

Uh. Better not say much. I don't think she ever knew that I knew. Go ahead, John, just be careful. "Aunt Billie, she fell. She died."

Mom nods. Silence reigns. Finally she speaks. "Surely you thought it was strange."

Being this close to the truth is making me nervous, more nervous than ever. "What?"

"My forbidding anyone to talk about that day."

Time for a who-cares gesture. I sigh, look away, and shrug.

"It was a trying time," Mom explains to Janet, "a trying experience, having Billie become so sick. I hate to admit this, but I was embarrassed. I didn't want to admit a family member could be mentally upset to the point of taking her life that way."

Janet has been stolid, blank. Now her face melts with compassion. "It can happen to anyone," she tells Mom. "In any family."

Mom doesn't look her way, amused that Janet doesn't yet get her point. Her eyes are on me as she says, "I know, Janet. That's why I'm so concerned about Johnny. He's deteriorating."

Before Janet can respond, I have my say. "Why didn't they do something?"

Upstairs, Ted's left his room, has used the bathroom. His steps – instead of tracing the path to his room, they've crossed the upper hallway and stopped at the top of the staircase. He's listening. The silence becomes thick as winter fog.

"Who? About what?" Mom asks. Her words display an uncharacteristic anxiety.

God, this is nerve-wracking. I'm dry as a powder keg. Need water. Unable to stand it any longer, I rise, shuffle hurriedly to a defensive position behind the rocker.

"Aunt Carol and Grandpa," I demand. "Why didn't they do something? They should have."

Mom's face is as blank as a wolf intent on her prey. She glances to Janet before she speaks. "Grandpa? He died two years before that, son. In the car wreck, remember? A careless driver crossed the centerline and hit him. A carbon copy of the one that hit me years later. Surely you remember."

No. This isn't happening. I'm losing it now, for sure. I see figments, all right? But I don't make mistakes like that. My memory is good, intact, as a matter of fact. She's lying. She's trying to make Janet believe I'm truly crazy and always have been. She wants control. She wants Ted.

Janet questions her about the wrecks. After a brief, noncommittal response, both turn my way. Now Janet's eyes are dark, glistening beads, housing the same blank stare as Mom's.

"Did you say Aunt Carol?" Mom asks.

I'm using my hands to rock the chair. Talk about nervous. "Yes! Aunt Carol, what about her?"

Silence, so palpable you can stir it.

"Son, you don't have an Aunt Carol."

Upstairs Ted moans. He's stomping his feet and crying. Screaming. He's swearing at the top of his lungs. He bounds down the stairs. Thump. Thump. Thump. He lunges toward me, stops cold, and drops to his knees, head to his palms. As he looks up, he's fixed on me, as if unaware of anyone else. "Please," he moans, "no more!"

SIX

"There, Janet," says Mom. "You see? Johnny's losing control. And Ted? Do you really want Johnny to have this sort of effect on him?"

Janet bends, sighs into her hands. Her defeat is now complete.

But why is it so stifling in here? Cool air from the open window's been flooding the room, curtains billowing. It should be pleasant. Oh. It's a tease, my biology telling me something better waits out there.

Janet lets out a breath and says, "I know. I try to do what's right, for both of them. But it's so hard." She throws herself into the couch's backrest, turns her back to me. The crying returns. It rises in pitch. She shakes all over.

I don't have an Aunt Carol? I never did? Why did Mom say that? In case anyone's wondering, I can prove Mom's wrong. All I have to do is pick up the phone book, look up Aunt Carol's number, and give her a call. In fact, she stopped by, oh, two, three weeks ago, while Janet was at work. If she were here now, she'd tell them.

And why's Ted looking around like that? Such anguish. It's as if he's been seeing an apparition of some sort, something frightening. All right, I have to face facts. My son's sick. He's inherited the one thing from me I can't possibly undo.

I remember that look of his, remember it from my own teen years. Sometimes I wouldn't be able to sleep, so I'd go to the bathroom, stare at myself in the mirror. As I think about it, my looks never changed much, although my reaction to what I saw did. So maybe the look I remember was an interpretation I superimposed on it that alternately frightened and fascinated. It was about that time that I noticed the symptoms Dr. Blucher badgers me about. And now Ted's inherited it. Schizophrenia.

No wonder Janet's been so distant. She knew, about Ted and me. She had to escape it somehow, and that's why she took solace in Evan Barnicke. I've been such a fool. I should have known.

I don't want to leave my place of refuge behind the rocking chair, but I have to. Can't stand Janet upset like this. Make it quick, John. Slip over to the couch.

Console her any way you can. After all, she's your lifeline. In a twinkling I'm on the couch, all over her, whispering, consoling.

Mom's silent for once, but I know she's agitated. Her constant shifting in that old straight-back, caned chair has it creaking, something like the house timbers' groans as they cool.

"Please, Dad," says Ted. "Please."

Janet's quieter now. Take care of Ted, John. You're his father. You know how. One slow, lurching move, and I'm at his side, turned so I can watch Mom, so I can make sure she doesn't do anything crazy. Ted's been shedding silent tears, probably afraid to cry aloud, afraid Mom will take the new clothes away. Sitting on my heels, my arms around him, he gives, melts into me. Strange, the way he's been steering clear of me for days, weeks, it seems. But now he's clinging, unusually warm, his tears hot and sticky on my rough cheek.

Is he sick, physically, I mean? No, I don't think so. He's distraught, and with good reason. At least I think that's it, what with Mom and Janet hovering, and then what I've put him through. Better talk to him. It's so hard, though. Hard to pull that sort of tenderness from my own inner dregs. It's as if my humanity's long since been sucked away, leaving this hulking shell of what once was. Have to do it, though. Have to do it for Ted. Don't really know where to begin, so I ask, "What is it, son?"

"Please," he says again. He pushes away and bends before me, talks into the floor. "I don't want you to be like this."

A lump forms in my throat. I haven't felt this much grief in a long time. "I'm sorry. I never wanted to be sick. I never wanted to be a problem. Not to you, and not to your Mom."

He jerks erect, freezes, eyes flitting about, almost as if he senses a ghost dancing about in the den's eerie light. Then his expression hardens, anger spewing from his eyes. "You have to stop, you have to stop doing this!" A stifled sob, fists clenched. He waves his arms in a frantic effort to include Mom, Janet, the house. "Why can't you just leave it alone?"

Leave it alone? Oh. He means I have to stop pretending I'm not sick. That I have to quit wishing things were normal for him again, the way they were when he was little, when Janet and I would play records and he'd dance with us.

"I wish things weren't this way, Ted. I wish I could do something to make it better for you." My eyes are wet now. My heart aches for him.

A fragile, fleeting smile breaks his tense expression. He reaches, his hand heavy on my arm. "It's not me, Dad. I'm not the problem. It's you. It's just that, like, you scare me sometimes."

Sitting this way has cramped me, so I grunt, flop to one side, pull into a cross-legged position. My legs are tingling. I rub them. Ted grabs one of my feet, pulls away the shoe, and rubs it while I'm working the kinks out of the other. It's an awkward, intimate moment. We laugh. Two comrades caught in the same predicament, managing to make the best of things.

"I don't mean to scare you," I tell him as I put on my shoes.

He looks down. "It's okay."

"No. No, it's not. I understand, that's all I'm saying."

A quizzical look. He squirms away. "What do you mean?"

Is it necessary to put it out there, in plain language? Of course it is. That's been the problem all along. If I could've made the effort to communicate with him, with Janet, they'd more nearly understand. I have a disease, but I'm not helpless, or evil, or dangerous. It's just a disease. And now Ted's got it.

"It's just a disease," I explain. "You can't help it any more than I can. You inherited it from me. I'm sorry, Ted. I'm so sorry."

His eyes widen. He scrambles away. He sits on his haunches, eying me like a cornered animal. "No!" he shouts. "I keep telling you, you're the one who's sick."

I offer a hand. "It's all right. I'll get help. Somehow I'll get help for you."

Now he's afraid, really afraid. But why? I'm only offering consolation. What is it he's afraid of? Doesn't he see this isn't the end of the line? He pushes himself erect, takes a faltering step back, circles the couch and dashes to the kitchen.

That's a new wrinkle. You'd think he'd have fled to his room, the way he usually does.

Mom's chair has stopped squeaking. She sits in her usual austere, rigid way, home to a painted frown. "I hope you're happy," she says. "I think you've finally pushed him over the edge. I'd better see to him."

I'm so embarrassed. When things quieten, I'll reconstruct what I've said and done, but I'm sure it's nothing. She's trying to push Janet and me into some exaggerated emotional response to Ted's problems. She's hoping we'll scare him away. But I'm on to her now. Still, it's embarrassing, having to deal with my peccadilloes this way, with her around to judge me.

"No," I tell her, "I'll go. He'll listen. Didn't you see? We were talking."

She laughs, an incredulous thread running through it. "Of course I saw. After what you just said, why do you think anyone other than I can help?" She pushes to her feet, rubs her neck, tests her legs, and strides toward the kitchen, where Ted's opening doors and drawers, clattering things. Rising, I mean to follow.

"John," Janet whispers, panicked, "please, let it go."

What? She's going along with Mom? Well, look at her. Those blank eyes, so intent. And her face. The encroaching crow's feet have disappeared. Her cheeks and forehead, they're as smooth as the lake on a calm day. Glassine. Is this the way she really looks? No, it's some figment, superimposed. Something else to tell Dr. Blucher about.

Mom and Ted have been shouting in the kitchen, but their row has now calmed. Mom strides around the corner and into the den, takes a seat next to Janet on the couch. I move to the rocker and sit. They've bent forward and are peering at me, two pairs of glassine, predator eyes. All right, I have to face this, whatever it is. Get it over with. Then help Ted.

Mom sighs, rubs her hands together. She's staring at me expectantly. Turn away, John.

The hawks are calling from the lake. "Come, John. Come!" I want to, I really do. A glance to the window. Pop the screen off, out into the yard. I can be at the cliffs in minutes. No, I have to exercise discipline. I have to see this thing through with Mom, get through to Janet, try to calm Ted. "I'm okay," I once more tell Mom. "I see figments, but I take medicine for it. Dr. Blucher says it's a slippery slope, but he knows I'm not unbalanced. I'll get better, you'll see."

"No, son, you won't. Your care isn't sufficient. It's outdated."

A glance toward Janet, who has turned completely porcelain. Still, those eyes, they're boring into me, into my innermost reaches, places I don't dare look myself. "No," I repeat. "You want to lock me away, in a sanitarium."

Something's happening at the window. Not noise, but movement. I can't look. I have to maintain this train of thought.

Carly's eyes flit toward Mom. "So this is super-bitch," she says.

"Quiet, sister," says Lana.

No. I can't deal with them now. Still, their presence compels, and I turn. Lana and Carly are standing guard over Michael and Vince, who don't seem to be aware of these two sexy female apparitions. Wish I had that gift.

Mom continues, unable to conceal her usual stern mien. "There's been so much progress since Billie's illness. No more shock treatments. The medications are better. Your Dr. Blucher apparently isn't keeping up with the times. You're not smoking or taking drugs or drinking, and that's in your favor. You'd be better if the medications were right, but they're not. Surely you realize that."

I don't want to hear this. Lana's whispering something from across the room, something lewd. My heart's pounding. Move around, John.

"Baby…" goes Lana.

Carly laughs. Vince adjusts his ascot. Michael's sitting on the windowsill, his Mickey Mouse legs swinging.

Then Carly begins making orgasm sounds, those whimpers and moans she gives off when Lana and I are doing…what? We don't have sex, so what is it? Carly makes those sounds while Lana and I…?

Mom's still talking, something about new treatments. She admits I'm not violent, that I'm not suicidal. "Your Dr. Blucher," she says, "has given you Droperidol, then Haloperidol, the older drugs. They control dopamine in your brain. But there's a newer drug out, Clozapine. It controls both dopamine and serotonin. It tends to a broader spectrum of symptoms."

"No more medicines," I protest softly, pedaling the rocker back a foot or two. Besides, I know about Clozapine; I've investigated it on the Internet. "Those drugs are bad, really bad. They're awful, debilitating. They're mind control." Twist in your seat, John, stomp your feet. Anything to get rid of this nervous tension. You can outlast her. You can. Stomp. Stomp!

"Your Mom's looked into this," says Janet, ignoring my antics. "Why don't we give it a try?" She blinks her glassy eyes.

Mom nods. "There've been so many advances," she repeats. "I know a doctor in Atlanta; he's a fine man, a former deacon in my church. Would you like me to call?"

Janet rises, approaches, then steps behind me. My shoes shuffle like crazy, sounding like fine sandpaper on the floor. The right hand begins to twitch, then the left. Mouth dry. Water. Her hands are on my shoulders. Normally they're warm, calming, but not now. She bends to my ear, her breath without its usual dampness. There's something wrong here. She whispers, "Please, John, for Ted."

Mom's been watching. Her eyes have followed Janet as she crossed the floor. She nods, as if approving of what Janet has just whispered. "Where was I?" Mom says. "Oh, yes. Dr. Sandifer. He comes highly recommended, Johnny. I know he can help."

"No," I whisper, trying to rein in my fear of what will come of her suggestion. A new doctor, new medications. No, I can't do that. I won't. Shake your head, John, show her you mean business. "I'm not going to a sanitarium. I'm not going to let you push me off a cliff."

None of this fazes Janet. She's gone over to the dark side. She's going to help Mom put me away, so she and Evan Barnicke can continue their affair. And Mom wants Ted. I'm their only obstacle. But I'm resolved. I won't cooperate.

Janet sighs, returns to the couch. Mom faces her. Thank God. Those two sets of eyes, they're finally off me. "I understand John's reluctance, though," Janet says. "He's an artist, a writer." She glances my way, as if to be assured I'm not going to speak for myself. Once more, my shoes begin their sandpapering. "He's so creative," she goes on. "That makes for a difficult life under any conditions, but especially with his schizophrenia. He's beginning to work again, and we need the money. But I think he's afraid this sort of change will upset his ability to work." She rolls her shoulders, the way Mom does, and again glances my way. "Normal society doesn't understand his kind of work. You have to write when inspiration hits. It doesn't happen every day."

What's this? Their faces have changed slightly. They could be sisters. No, identical twins, only one has gray hair, the other red. So strange. But does this mean that, despite Janet's momentary sympathy, she's still not on my side?

"Of course," Mom replies. An oddly sympathetic sheen floods her flesh-eater eyes, transforming them to green. She nods, her straight, shoulder-length hair swaying in relentless, ordered movement, like columns of emaciated, close-quartered soldiers on the march. "But you do understand, this goes beyond artistic eccentricity."

"Yes," Janet says. She sniffs, pulls a tissue from a pants pocket and daubs at the ceramic flesh below her eyes.

"Something has to be done, and soon," Mom reiterates, a determined edge to her voice. She reaches, pats Janet's hand, a gesture I would never have thought her capable of. "Look, Dr. Sandifer works part-time through a state-run clinic, where money's available for treatment. So, really, you have nothing to lose. I can virtually guarantee he'll improve under Dr. Sandifer. They have rooms at the state clinic, where John can stay until he's stabilized on the medication."

Janet shrugs and nods. Mom's victory is now irrevocable. They're going to lock me away. Both turn toward me, faces hard as glass, eyes boring holes in me.

After a minute or so, Janet blinks. "Please, John?"

Eons pass. I'm still nervous, maybe a bit addled, I admit. To relieve the tension, I stomp my feet again. "What?" I demand from my perch on the rocker, louder than appropriate, very loud, actually. "What exactly is it you want?"

Oh. Janet's porcelain features begin to flake, scale-like, surely a grotesquerie I could never have conjured.

"Quit it!" Ted screams from the kitchen, the word slurred. "Shut up!" Whatever the commotion is he's now involved in, it's growing louder. "I won't live like this anymore," he yells, "I won't!"

"There, you see?" Janet says, her voice now a deep growl. "Is this what you want? Do you want Ted to be so afraid of you that he won't want to live with us?"

"Sheee-it!" yells Carly. "C'mon, Vince, let's party!"

Vince sniffs. "I don't care a damn for your attitude, girlfriend."

Carly responds with a yell, which makes Vince sway, as if caught in a gale. "Asshole!" she shouts, then lunges for him. He sidesteps her. From a safe distance, he brushes at his jacket, fluffs his ascot. Lana grabs Carly, and so does Michael. Michael, poor little fellow, loses his grip and falls in a pile to the floor. He looks hurt.

Carly, eyes on Vince, wriggles free of Lana, reels toward him. "I have a bone to pick with you, dipwad. Without those fancy clothes, you'd be nothing, do you hear me? Nothing!" She lunges. "I'll rip those pussy clothes off you!"

Lana grabs her, holds her.

But that dust-up isn't my concern. It's Ted. The commotion in the kitchen has stopped, and I feel him staring at me. I turn to discover him peeking from inside the kitchen like a glowering Kilroy.

What's this? I can see him, really see into him, as if for the first time, to the source of his pain. The angry fever swelling in his eyes begins to fill mine. I can't have this, I have to maintain equanimity. Turn away, John. As I do, Ted swears and slips back into the kitchen.

Janet rises again, nears, reaches for me, her face a crusty, flaking egg. I motion her away.

A crash from the kitchen, a chair, I think. Dishes clatter and smash. Ted's swearing at the top of his lungs. Something falls, something massive. Mom rises, turns abruptly toward the kitchen noise, her face alligatored with cracks in jagged, hexagonal shapes. A piece falls from her left cheek. Beneath, there's hair, wolf's hair. Am I hearing growls from her now? It's hard to tell, because Carly's shrieking. She begins a belly dance. Vince bows to Lana, and they swing into a waltz, oddly in sync with Carly.

"Ted!" Mom yells. "Stop it! This instant!"

"Fuck you!" Ted bellows.

She stalks toward him, her hands doubling and re-doubling with each step. I twist, watch until she wheels into the kitchen. Their yelling turns to white noise. I slump from the rocker to the floor, on my knees, then to all fours. This has to stop. This is insane. And they think I'm crazy?

Oh. The television's still on. It's muted, but the invasion of Iraq has finally started. Tanks are moving in echelons, the invasion's spearhead. The programming switches to Baghdad, where the sky once again strobes, as if home to a lightning storm. Buildings rattle. Dust boils skyward. Antiaircraft batteries send streams of red exclamations angling into the dark. You'd think the earth was engaged in combat with the sky.

Another switch. Back at the Kuwaiti border, someone waves, points toward Iraq's heartland. Soldiers run. A senior person standing on an armored vehicle makes sky –pointing circles with one hand, then pumps the hand. Dust begins to boil as phalanxes of armored personnel carriers jerk into gear and rumble into Iraq. Soon the TV screen is filled with them, and as the camera pans back, armored helicopters, bristling with weapons, emerge from the night and hover protectively overhead.

A scream from the kitchen. It's Mom. Ted bellows. More crashing. More yelling. I want to go there, stop the trouble, but I can't move. I'm immobilized, hardly able to breathe. Sweat begins to drip from my cheeks and chin. In the kitchen, Mom moans, as if she's been wounded. Ted bellows victoriously. What gives?

Janet motions me to stand. I comply, slowly, uncertainly. Still, I can't move toward the kitchen. I can't even move in her direction. She backs away and stands watching from arm's length, her face once again a porcelain spheroid, expressing nothing but calm curiosity. She holds one hand folded tightly over the other, waist-high.

The window. The one she left bare and partly open. She did this on purpose. She left me a way out. She's had to conspire against me with Mom, but she did it against her will, I know that now. She loves me. She really does love me.

Her ceramic face now shows visible cracks. It's coming apart, the way an egg might, giving birth to something…what? As the pieces fall, there's another, smaller Janet inside. It begins to crack. She speaks, but it's not her voice, it's some shrill, demonic wail, the words so distorted I can't make them out. She offers an equally ceramic hand.

No! The window. I find I can move in that direction. Don't know how Janet knew this was my only remaining option — I'll have to think it through later. But now I know what I have to do. It's the only way. The lake. That's what this strange day has been about. The cliffs. Of course. I've been resisting it all day. My refuge is at the cliffs. My salvation. Dad. I understand now, Dad. I know why you did it, although I know I'll never opt out the way you did. When I get to the cliffs, everything will somehow be better. Okay, then. Oh. The action on TV — berserk!

Bombs rain on Baghdad. I can't see their descent, but flashes of light precede the muffled thumps. The bombs, they begin to pound in my temple. Buildings mushroom outward and sink in slow collapse.

Another segue. The armored invasion's spearhead meets its first resistance — a line of dug-in tanks, reinforced by sandbagged mortar positions, Iraqi soldiers shouldering rocket propelled grenades. The fighting is fierce. Allied tanks veer crazily about. Armored helicopters dart in, fire, bounce, then zip away — a swarm of angry metal hornets. In a few more minutes, the Iraqi position is overrun, and the phalanx moves on.

Oh. The window. Two, three steps, and I'm there. My fingers are like stumps as I try to unfasten the screen. There. It's gone, into the night's abyss.

Mom wails. By the sound of it, she's stumbling through the kitchen. I'm about to push one leg out the window, but her moans are calling. I look back. She's covered with blood, a towel wrapped around her arm, face stricken and mournful. She stops, peels the towel away, revealing a nasty gash. A vein has been opened. Blood spasms from it.

Ted. He rounds the corner, a bloody butcher knife in one hand, raised high. Apparently done with Mom, he turns his deranged look to me. No. Not Ted. Not my son. He wouldn't do this. No!

Janet backs in horror toward the couch, trips, falls into its cushions. She looks away from Ted, to me.

But I have to go. The lake, the cliffs. A glance into the night tells me everything there is quiet, serene, not like this. DeSade would be at home here, but not me.
More shuffling, rapid-fire words, then shouts. One more look back.

Janet's chest is open, a long gash showing through her blouse. It's turning red, a crimson tide, spreading like cancer.

Ted spins. He's almost to me. He breathes in short, shallow gasps.

What can I do? Press against the windowsill, John, pull that leg in. Defend yourself. If you can overwhelm him, maybe you can calm him, maybe reason this attack away.

The knife's long blade glints as it sweeps toward my chest. I evade the thrust and grab, as if under military control. I have his wrist.

"Bastard!" he screams. "Motherfucker!" He kicks, but not high enough to hit my crotch.

Ow! My knee, he got my knee. My grip on his wrist weakens. He jerks loose.

"Ted!" Janet gasps weakly, barely able to breathe. Ted has apparently punctured one of her lungs. "Please!"

Mom careens to the couch, falls beside Janet, the arm and towel pressed against Janet's abdomen. "I can stop the bleeding, Janet," she says, her authoritative manner now returned, "but you have to stay calm. Here." With her free hand, she jams a couch cushion against Janet's wound.

The knife blade arcs toward me again. This time I grab Ted's arm above the elbow. Squeeze, John, pull, hard.

Ted writhes, turns. His arm tenses with the pressure. "Cocksucker!" he yells. Then his bony shoulder shakes and snaps, dislocated at an ugly angle. He shudders, an awful cry escaping him. He falls limp.

My God, his shoulder is ruined. I did that, to my son. To Ted, whom I love more than anyone in the world, maybe even more than Janet. But I have to go. I have to get to the lake, to the cliffs. Then I can think things through. Hear the hawks?

"Cree-dom! Cree-dom!" they're calling.

That's it. That's where my freedom lies. Not here. Not in the attic. Not on TV. Not with Janet. On the cliffs, on this cool, dark, quiet night.

There. My feet are on the ground. It's solid, reassuring. Stop, John. Listen.

There's no sound from inside the house. Are Mom and Janet dead? Has Ted passed out? His arm and shoulder, they must hurt awfully. I'm so sorry, I didn't mean to do it, Ted, but you had a knife. I had to do something. Something bad lives in that house, something evil. I have to get away. I have to.

Five steps, and I'm to the edge of the woods. Now forty, fifty steps. I'm hopelessly lost. Which way is the lake? I can't tell. Nothing to do but retrace my steps, find Ted. See to him. Watch out! Snakes on the branches. What am I to do? I can't go on. Oh! Trip, fall. A pile of leaves cushions my collapse. It's over. The lake, the cliffs, I guess they were only a lure, something to get me out of the house. What do I do now? So tired. At least I'm out of danger. All I needed was to get out of that awful house. So tired. Have to see about Ted. Janet's no good, she's porcelain. And Mom, we know what she is. The leaves, they're soft and cooling against my face. That's it, rest. Close your eyes, John, a strange, new voice tells me. Sleep.

What time is it? How long have I been asleep? And what's this? A police car is idling in the drive, an EM vehicle, too. The outside house lights are on, illuminating the alien vehicles. The police radio squawks like some mechanical bird talking to the night. This is about Ted, surely.

Now I can tell where I am. I'm fifty long steps from the house. The window remains open wide, its screen at a cockeyed angle against the house, Janet's curtains now luffing outward. They could just as well be wings, something inside the house trying to fly to the cliffs, to escape the invisible, inner oppression the house represents.

Two cops are walking about inside the house, looking down. One, a stout fellow, stoops, rises, writes in a tiny notebook. He nods as someone else speaks, and then he writes some more. The other cop seems a lot younger. This one looks to the window, approaches it, peers into the night. I'm still concealed, though. He can't see me this deep in the woods.

But I have to get closer and find out what's going on. What if this is another figment, the most complex, the most real one yet? How will I be able to tell? So confusing.

"It's okay, baby," says Lana, who has somehow found me, her voice so soft, so intimate. "You stay here. I'll sneak a peek."

I'm sweating, despite the nighttime cooling. A drop slips past one eye, runs down my cheek and drips, splats on a brittle leaf. Lana's right, I can't be the one to assess what's going on. It has to be her. "Okay," I say, "you go."

Amazing how quickly she can cover ground. She crouches beneath the window, catlike, alert. No Special Forces operative could work as effectively. For some reason, I want to emulate her. Rising, I stumble forward, step into the clearing. She extends a palm to stop me, indicates with walking fingers for me to go back, remain hidden. She points to herself, then levels two forked fingers before her eyes, points to the window to tell me she's going to look inside.

Okay, I nod, and retreat to the tree line. She rises, peers inside.

For what seems an eternity, she watches, listens. Her lithe body remains tensed. She could be a reared mountain lion about to attack. Finally she bends, looks about and lopes toward me. So silent. So agile.

She knows Ted; we talk about him all the time. But she says she doesn't know these other people.

"They're cops," I tell her.

She frowns. "But two are wearing white outfits."

"Those are probably EMTs. Emergency Medical."

Her eyes widen as understanding dawns.

"Who else?" I ask.

"Just Ted."

"What about Mom? And Janet?"

She hugs her shoulders against the night chill, the way Janet does. Moonlight filters through the trees, still strong enough to reveal the amusement shining in her eyes. "Nope," she says, the word firm, final.

I swallow, lick my too-dry lips. "I don't understand. They should be there. The EMTs must have come for them. Ted stabbed them. Blood was everywhere. Maybe they're already in the EM vehicle."

Now her amusement grows to a smile of the I-know-something-you-don't variety. "Okay," she says, her voice rising half an octave as the word passes from her, "see for yourself."

No. I can't do it. I don't ever want to be near that house again. But something inside me is screaming, "Yes! Do it, John." So I have to. I have to.

I close my eyes, rehearse how I'll emulate Lana's approach. Then I'm off, controlled completely by the body, by instinct. I've forgotten to count steps, but that's okay. I'm below the window, one hand on the house's damp siding. Lana gives me a thumbs up.

Gosh. Her dress is nothing but a film, a transparency, moonlight silhouetting her slender body. No. Don't think about that. Ted. Find out about Ted. Mom. Janet.

Inside, Ted's been strapped to a board on a stretcher, the dislocated arm bound to his side. His eyes seem flat, vacant. They must've given him a painkiller. He mumbles some drawn-out rant, but the words are too slurred to comprehend. His shirt – it should be blood-soaked, but there's no sign. The couch, too, it should be covered with Mom's and Janet's blood. Nothing. The knife's on the coffee table. Someone must've wiped the blood from it.

The two cops stand before Ted. The burly cop who was writing, he's bald with a thick neck, and he wears sergeant's stripes on his blue-gray uniform. His arms, face and neck glisten, as if he's been sweating. The other cop is taller, black hair cropped short on the sides, parted neatly on top. He's a shade over six feet and holding a thermal-paper coffee cup. He looks hardly older than Ted.

Behind them, a pair of EMTs watch. One, with arms crossed over his chest, seems about to laugh. One corner of his black mustache is cocked high, his swarthy face wrinkled with amusement.

The sergeant turns to him. "What the hell did you give him? He incoherent."

"He's drunk, Sarge," the black mustachioed EMT replies. "Can't you smell it?"

The other EMT, a short, black man with a pencil-thin mustache, waggles a thumb toward the kitchen. "Killed a pint of Jack Black, from the looks of it. Had it hidden in the kitchen. Tore the whole damn place up looking for it. Then got drunk as a coot. I had to give him some Thorazine to calm him down."

"Let's give him some coffee, wake him up," the younger cop says to Black Mustache.

The EMTs lift the stretcher at one end, raising Ted's head a foot or so. Ted takes in a long sip of the cop's coffee, then another.

"All right," Sarge tells Ted, "start over. Tell us what happened."

Ted blinks. His eyes regain their focus, and he looks from face to face. "My dad," he says with slurred words, "he's nuts."

"I got that much," says Sarge. He looks around. "And where is this dad of yours?"

"I told you. He broke my arm. Then he climbed through that window. He ran."

The younger cop steps forward. "We looked for him all over, even outside. He ain't nowhere about, if there is such a person." He gestures toward the coffee table. "What about that knife? You said something about a knife when you called. Is that the one, there on the coffee table?"

Sarge waves him to silence, pokes Ted with his shoe to keep him from drowsing. "All right, you called 911. You said your dad broke your arm. Why'd he do that?"

Ted grimaces for a moment and looks away. "I was going to kill him."

Dead silence. Then the four men shuffle their feet. I can tell it's disconcerting for them. For me, it's a nightmare to hear such words from my son.

"Okay," says Sarge.

With difficulty, Ted once again tries to explain. "He's schizophrenic. Mom divorced him a couple of years ago. She married her boss and moved to Atlanta. She didn't want me, so the judge, he left me with Dad. I didn't have anywhere else to go."

"Schizophrenic?" Black Mustache says. "Was he on medication?"

"Sometimes. He had a prescription. Didn't take it much."

"He saw things? He had hallucinations?"

"I don't know. Maybe. Yeah. He kept telling me he and Mom were doing things. She called me earlier today, said she might stop by for a minute. The first time in two years. I ran all the way out to the main road looking for her, but she didn't come."

"Did he think she was coming?" Sarge asks.

Ted nods. Then his eyes roll sleepily. "He was afraid Grandma would come, too, and put him away."

"Okay," Sarge says, "so why did you need to stab him?"

Ted blinks, swallows. "He was freaking me out." His voice is weak now, and he shakes his head. "I just wanted him to stop being nuts."

Sarge takes the spiral-bound pad from his chest pocket and scribbles. "You mentioned your grandma. Where does she live?"

"She died in a car crash a year before the divorce. Head-on."

Sarge looks to Black Mustache.

"Possible," says the EMC. "Schizophrenics can hold onto stuff like that."

Sarge drops to one knee before Ted. "So you live here with your dad. Your mom and grandma are dead. He's all you have?"

"Yeah. No. I don't have him anymore. Not anymore. Maybe I'll go live with my friend Jimmy. His mom said I could. I've been sleeping in the woods some so I don't have to be around Dad. Sometimes, like last night, I go to Jimmy's."

"You go to school?"

"Sometimes."

"Why sometimes?"

Ted's lower lip trembles, his eyes are red, glassy. He begins to cry.

"You okay?" Sarge asks.

"Better give him another shot," says Black Mustache.

"Not yet." Sarge bends low. "Okay, son, why do you only go to school sometimes?"

Ted's bawling. He turns away.

"Come on, kid, tell me what's going on."

"I'm schizophrenic!" Ted screams.

Sarge jerks to his feet, steps away. "What the hell." He glances to Black Mustache.

"It happens," says the EMC. "People can inherit it."

The younger cop is wide-eyed. "This is weird," he whispers. "This is way weird."

Black Mustache kneels. "You been diagnosed?"

"No." Ted chokes off a sob. "But Dad keeps telling me I am, so I must be. Sometimes I see things. I see Mom. Tonight I saw Grandma, too, but only a couple of times. Mostly I know better, but I'm getting like him, I know I am."

"This been going on long?" Black Mustache asks.

"Maybe a year."

The swarthy EMT turns to Sarge. "We got no place for something like this. "We'll have to take him to Grady Memorial in Atlanta."

Sarge pokes his forehead with the butt end of his pen, makes a few more notes. "All right, get him out of here. Archie, bag that knife."

The EMTs lift the stretcher, carry Ted away. The younger cop tugs a clear plastic bag from a back pocket, nudges the knife into it.

The whole scene has mesmerized me. I don't know. I don't. Is this something else I created? Nothing about it makes sense. Nothing. I crouch, lean against the house, softly sobbing.

"It's okay, baby," says Lana.

She's beside me now. I glance up. She peers deeply into my hurt, but for once it doesn't feel like a violation.

"Janet's gone? And Mom?"

"I'm sorry," she says. "I wanted to tell you. We all did. But you wouldn't let us."

"Just me and Ted. We're all that's left."

"Well, not exactly. There's Carly, and me, and all the rest."

"Figments."

"If you say so, John." She chokes on the words, her eyes swelling. She's hurt that I would say such a thing.

We work our way past our divergent emotions. The night has cooled my sweat. I feel goose bumps forming. Lana, now that her emotional moment is over, seems crisp, bright, unaffected.

"Come on," she says. "Let's go to the lake. The others are waiting. We're going to make a night of it there."

We rise together, turn toward the woods. At the tree line, she takes the lead. She strides off, on a path I've never taken before. We're trotting now, the night breathing softly about us. It's easy this way, on this path. There're no snakes, and the path's a wide one. Why is it I've never found it?

I begin to laugh. Lana stops, turns, circles to my rear, her odd expression reflecting the moon's soft light. She approaches, puts a finger to my lips.

Strange. For the first time I can feel her touch. Sensing it, she cradles my face in her palms, kisses me, the way she's done so many times before. But this time her lips are warm, the way Janet's have always been. I take her in my arms, lift her to her toes, return the kiss.

We break. She's so light, as light as Ted when he was maybe two years old. She glances up, and then turns shyly away. So much like Janet.

"You okay?" I ask.

A giggle. "Of course. You?"

Am I? Suddenly I feel giddy, elated and sad at the same time, but as though a load has been taken off me. "Yes. I think so."

"You get it, then?"

"Get it?"

"About all this. You know, Janet and Mom, and this thing tonight with Ted. The cops and EMTs. The whole scene."

I have to think that one over. Looking through the window, hearing all that. Unreal. That's the only way I can describe it. Life, it's so strange. It never reveals its twists and turns in concrete, reproducible ways. If, as Lana's implying, that wasn't real, then what is?

Ah. Something begins to dawn. Not a clear picture yet, hardly an epiphany, but some inner shift. It still makes little sense, but somehow I'm okay with it. All of it. And that includes my strange inner world.

"Yeah, I get it." I realize I really do. Reality is merely an evanescence we create for our own amusement.

We create it from what we believe should be true, a mirror image of the way I'd always been led to understand that reality and belief intertwine. Isn't that it?

Lana stands before me, hands on hips, head cocked to one side, giving me the enigmatic smile that so enthralls me. "To the cliffs?"

I smile and shrug.

She turns. Now we're running. I'm chasing her, laughing the way Ted might once have. She laughs, too, lets me catch up, teasingly, and then runs ahead. In no time, the trees are thinning. Now we're in a small clearing on the slope leading to the cliffs. The moon bobs for a moment atop them. As it rises, it sends a swollen reflection wriggling across the water toward us like a thousand eager, happy snakes.

I, SINGULARITY

You might think this posturing, but I never considered my blindness a liability. Fact is, I thrived in social situations. I had constant invites to parties, and for a while I was even considered something of a draw. A cliché, I know, but at a young age I came to realize that my remaining senses more than compensated for the lack of sight, and so at those later adult parties I was never a source of awkwardness or a magnet for sympathy. Sure, people would sometimes shake my hand and tell me how great it was to see me. Then, aware of their mini-faux pas, they'd go silent. But I'd just grin and say, Well, it's super to see you, too. C'mon, let's have some fun.

So party mingling was easy. Even within the din of music, clinking glasses, and conversation, footsteps provided an aural map to restrooms, doorways, the buffet table, and places to sit, and I always navigated without assistance. I had great, mischievous fun at parties, too. It was so easy to eavesdrop on conversations without fear of discovery, and then later, I could casually throw out those overheard items as gossipy tidbits, and that really got people's attention. Then, as I grew bolder, I found I could have even more fun – play the hyper-sensitive one with out-of-control drunks, shout them down and demand that they leave.

And my other senses – wow! An eminently refined sense of taste revealed *everything* about the hors d'oeuvres. Even with the subtlest blending of spices and other condiments, I could discern each dish's ingredients, their proportions and freshness. I would praise these treats when I knew they'd appeal to discriminating palates, and I always took it upon myself to inform the host of their shortcomings – in the most tactful manner, of course. And smell: I identified men by their mixture of musk and aftershave, women by their unique, slightly acidic scents, something perfume couldn't mask. A simple sniff, and there I'd be, calling out their names. The grip of a hand or a squeeze of my shoulder would tell me all I needed to know about those persons' reaction to my antics.

Invariably, someone would express amazement at my ability to pick out the foxiest women in the room, but with four senses working overtime, coupled with a lucid imagination and a formidable memory, why couldn't I? I always smiled at the undertone of concern buzzing about me when I asked a woman to dance, but once in motion, everyone seemed to realize that my feet had eyes of their own. It was this especially, I think, that made me seem someone people *had* to get to know.

But it was at home that my lack of sight became burdensome. During my early school years, as I'd listen to TV, my sister Tess would slide onto the couch beside me, run her fingers over the skin folds covering my eye sockets, and start to cry.

"Don't, Tess," I'd say. "Don't do that."

"What?"

"You heard me."

Then she'd moan softly and ask, "Does it hurt, Harold?"

"No," I'd say, loudly. She'd start bawling, Mom would come running, and I'd miss the rest of my TV show as we sorted things out. Meaning I'd try one more time to convince them I wasn't helpless, that I was as okay as they were.

So how had this blindness come about? Well, Grandma Beverly was pregnant with Mom, and a German immigrant doctor named Grünenthal gave her

Thalidomide for morning sickness. Massive doses, I'm told. That awful chemical didn't produce birth defects in Mom, but it apparently misinformed her genes, and I came out with these odd skin folds over my orbits, the ocular cavities that should have housed a pair of eyes. Mom screamed at Grandma, blaming her for my lack of sight. Gaining no satisfaction there, she took me to doctor after doctor, demanding that I be given a way of seeing. But scans confirmed that I had no ocular tissue and no neural connections to the brain, so vision wasn't possible.

During my early teen years, with Mom facing defeat after defeat in her battle to reward me with sight, I'd hear Dad and her talking about it after we were in bed. I'd first hear them mumbling about Tess. Then Mom would say in a higher, strained voice, Mark, what're we going to do about Harold's eyes? Dad would answer, He's a good-looking young man. He'd grow into a handsome adult if we could get those folds removed. But he wouldn't have eyes, Mom would reply, and she'd start crying. He could have prosthetic eyes embedded in his ocular cavities, Helen, Dad would say. No! Mom would cry out, I won't have him going about with glass eyes, looking like a zombie. Still, over time Mom came to grips with my lack of sight and Dad began to accept the skin folds as a natural part of my facial terrain.

I was never one to be intimidated by much of anything, and I began to leave the house for the streets. I couldn't drive, but there was always the bus to carry me wherever I wanted to go, so being out in public alone became second nature. Then a few years later, a month or so after I finished college, Mom and Dad died in a gang shooting at the mall, and for a long while Tess stayed holed up at nights in that drafty old house. For some reason, she started pestering me again about my lack of sight. One hand would cup my face and she'd say something totally lame like, "Oh, Harold, you don't have to run all over town to escape your blindness. Why won't you talk to me about it?"

Picture my teeth grinding here. "Damn it, Tess," I'd bellow, "I have been talking to you. As far as I'm concerned, I don't have a problem. I'm in control of my life. So what is it with you, are you jealous?"

Sometimes I wouldn't be paying enough attention after saying such things, and her slap would set my cheek on fire. Then I'd sense some slight motion of her hips on the couch cushions as she raised the hand again. I'd grab it. Let go of me, Harold! she'd yell as she jerked the hand away. Then she'd bolt upright and run crying to her room.

Finally one night she screeched, "All right, if you're so in control of your life, why are you still living here? I need to get on with my own life, and your being here isn't helping."

"Fine!" I yelled. "I'd jump at the chance to get away from you." She bawled then in a most disheartened way, and I finally realized I'd been an insensitive lout to her, well, since forever. "I'm sorry, Sis," I said, "I guess I should've moved out a long time ago, let you spread your wings a bit."

Still angry, she said, "Well, why didn't you?"

I whistled out a long sigh as I thought. "I guess change is hard for me."

Over the next few months, I backed out of one move after another, and every time I'd renege on my promise, we'd have another screaming match. Over time, our sibling bond grew strained to the breaking point. She'd throw things, mostly Mom's knickknacks. By then I'd learned to sense her arm in motion and could either deflect those dangerous, fragile porcelains or dodge them altogether. She'd storm out of the room, click-clack across the kitchen linoleum to the carpeted rear hallway. After a final blast of high-pitched name-calling, she'd slam her bedroom door, and that night's bout would be over. Then I'd make a few phone calls, locate a party, and forget Tess.

But as we kept up those scraps, I began to notice my pulse pounding, my breathing coming in gasps. I'd sweat copiously. Then the headaches. The throbbing would begin in my temples, something I could massage away while taking a few deep breaths. As time passed, though, the throbs spread across my forehead. Massaging them away became impossible, so I'd pat a warm washcloth onto my forehead, and after a half-hour of lying on my bed in a trance-like state, the pain would ease. More fights, louder screaming, and the throbbing began to coalesce at my forehead's center. The headaches grew deeper and would last all day and night, depriving me of sleep.

Desperate for relief, I made an appointment with Doctor Wentz.

"Very strange," he said as he took in the MRI films. "Your orbits are filling up with tissue."

Wonderful, I thought. Just great. Really.

"It must be a psychosomatic mechanism caused by the headaches," he said. "Frankly, I don't see any cause for worry – about *that*."

Something else? I had no desire to cope with yet more physiological oddities and still more change.

He gently tapped a tender place at the midpoint of my forehead. "There seems to be something significant going on here."

By that time, my ability to visualize had almost disappeared; consequently, my social life had become a disaster. Could the headaches – and my scraps with Tess – be destroying my imagination? I wondered. Was my vaunted, life-of-the-party manner going the way of the Dodo bird? "A tumor, doc? Cancer? What?"

"A lump beneath the epidermis, maybe a cyst. I'm sure it's nothing to worry about." He patted my shoulder. "But we'll keep an eye on it." Then, realizing his gauche idiom, he coughed and began scribbling.

This new development sent my relationship with Tess off on a slightly different heading. Her concern plummeted to something akin to commiseration – as if she suffered deformations like mine – and my irritation with her grew beyond bounds. The cyst-like tissue at the center of my forehead matured quickly after that, the spot ultra-sensitive. As our feuds reached a new crescendo, I decided to move into an apartment on the bus line, and we kissed each other off for good. The headaches continued, and another doctor visit followed a second MRI.

Doctor Wentz blew out a breath, an uncharacteristic response from this most placid of doctors. "Harold, I think it's time to cut the skin and take a look at that lump on your forehead."

That's all he'd say about it, and I objected, strenuously. In the persistent way of physicians, he won me over without giving up a lot of details, and so yesterday morning he attended while a plastic surgeon performed the operation. When I came to, my senses seemed a worse mess than usual. Maybe it was the lingering effects of anesthesia, but I couldn't make out a damned thing. Sure, I heard clatters and footfalls, and the astringent hospital smells hovered everywhere in the too-cool air, the dry, chemical, post-op taste unavoidable, but I couldn't remotely shape those sensations into the mental images that have always helped me navigate life. For the first time ever, I was claustrophobic over my lack of sight. I screamed. I kept screaming.

Finally, Doctor Wentz pressed a hand to my mouth. "Harold," he said, "I want you to try to see."

I shoved the hand away. "Are you freaking nuts? I'm blind!"

Then a familiar, feminine sob. Tess? What was she doing there?

"Please," she said, her shoes tap-tapping. "Please try to see, Harold. For me."

Piling on, Doctor Wentz said, "Your sister had a call from your workplace that you were having surgery, they told her it was, serious. She's been here all morning. She wanted to make sure you were going to be all right."

My sis. Ever the bleeding heart. Well, I had no idea what it would be like to see in the normal sense, but I tried. A spasm of some sort rippled at the center of my forehead. Then it occurred again, and I sensed the skin flap over the spot on my forehead moving. That time I had the sensation of light. Not the refined, inner light I was used to, but a harsh glare. Images of human forms appeared, much cruder than I'd imagined them.

Doctor Wentz smiled, an animalistic expression, it seemed. "The lump on your forehead," he said, "was an eye forming. It's something unheard of in medical science, something we can only call a singularity. You body has continued to adjust to the Thalidomide, and I'm positive that a primary part of it has been this adjustment to your lack of sight." He glanced to a freakish, robotic-looking Tess. She sobbed quietly, still tap-tapping. What with my resisting the few moments of physical tenderness we'd shared over the years, I'd never noticed that she had no ears, only tiny, almond-shaped holes for hearing, that she had to move her head to and fro in order to hear clearly.

Such a freakout! I could hardly breathe. My new eye clamped shut. I didn't want this, I wanted things the way they were. Even Tess, I wanted her undeformed, as I'd always assumed she was. Then I began to convulse again. Doctor Wentz bent, cigarette breath engulfing me, and as he restrained me I noticed my old, enhanced senses returning. They pulsed to full sentience. I tried to open my eye again, tried to see one last time. I couldn't. Doctor Wentz said something about a sedative. The IV tube taped to my hand plumped, and an icy feeling surged toward my elbow. The convulsions calmed. He and Tess began talking to one another, but their voices seemed far away, dream-like. As the sedative continued its work, a thought came: I'm a singularity, Doctor Wentz had said. I'm unique. Well, I've always known that.

THE PHANTOM

What's the deal with this baseball, you ask? Well, you may not remember, but it's one Grandpa gave me back in the day. And why do I keep toying with it? Say, here's an idea. We have a nice Indian summer day on our hands, and Janice took the grandkids on an all-day to the fair, so why don't I help you out to the patio and I'll tell you all about it.

Settled in? Good. Here's a second cup for you. Okay, so here's the way it happened.

Grandpa had taken a few days off from that Augusta textile mill where he worked – he was a mechanic there, if you recall. Well, he'd ridden the bus to Atlanta to visit us, but first he wanted to watch the Crackers play the Birmingham Barons at that old ballpark. As he told me the story a couple of days later, the bus made a lot of stops along the way, and the driver was poking along slow as

Christmas, and when they stopped there on Ponce de Leon Avenue, game time was only a few minutes away.

So he gets off, looks across the street at the long ticket line. Someone there was hollering that bleacher seats were the only ones available. Grandpa would never sit that far away from the action, so he decides to bag that day's game. But since he's in Atlanta he ducks into the Sears Roebuck across from the ballpark to see if he can get a deal on a new pair of work boots. He finds a pair in his size, puts them on layaway, and on the way out he remembers my birthday was the previous week.

What? You've really forgotten my birth date, big brother? All those years on the high seas would let you forget a few family things, I guess. It's the fifth of August, right after... What? How could you remember Grandpa's visit that weekend and not remember I'd just had a birthday? Oh, that's right, you showed up on leave from the Navy right after dinner, and Mom was still giving Grandpa what-for for popping in unannounced. She'd been on him about taking a bath, too, and he still hadn't done that. It was hot on buses in the summertime back then, and Grandpa had sweated a lot and, what with the whiskey he'd been drinking on the bus, he did smell kind of ripe.

Anyway, he's headed out of Sears, and he wants to buy tickets for the whole family for the next day's game, as well as some sort of present for me, but he doesn't come close to having enough money. So he takes the trolley home and tells Mom he's put his first pair of new boots in five years on layaway, and after the down payment he doesn't have enough money for tickets for all of us for the next day's game, and he wants to buy me that post-birthday present, too, so can he borrow a few bucks until his next paycheck, pretty please? You know, put the old fatherly charm on her. Even tries to hug her, smelly as he is. She shoves him away and doesn't even ask how much. She snatches a handful of bills from her purse and shoves them at him. He takes the trolley back to the ballpark, buys the tickets and, realizing she's handed him way too much money, he ducks into Sears again and picks up his boots. So his story goes, he's a little woozy from the long ride and the drinking and having not eaten all day, and he gets lost trying to find his way out. Ends up in the sports department. He still has some money left over and he decides to buy me some baseball-related thing for my birthday.

The ball? Looks new, doesn't it? No, actually, I did use it, a lot. No, really, I did. But let me go on, okay?

So he starts looking around, and he notices a stacked pyramid of packaged baseballs on the floor. Some are Wilsons, others are Rawlingses, and there are a couple of cheap off-brands, too. He's sort of staring at the pile when one of the boxes on a lower layer flops open and a ball tumbles out. He picks it up and looks it over, and there isn't a brand on it – it's a plain baseball.

But it isn't exactly plain, as you can see. The stitches are tight, extremely tight, and in this shade of blue, a color of baseball thread I've never seen since. Smell it. See? It smells like new horsehide, doesn't it? You can dent it with a fingernail and you can wet it, or rub dirt on it, but it won't stain or scuff. Here's my pocketknife. Just try and cut it. See? Not a mark, even after all these years.

Well, the floor manager's hanging around, watching, and Grandpa thinks the guy might be assuming he's planning to steal it, so he walks over, shows it to the man, and points to the empty box. The floor manager rolls his eyes and says he can't keep it in its box. Whenever someone stops there, he tells Grandpa, it bounces over like a puppy begging to be taken home.

Then Grandpa says, "I don't see a brand on it."

"It's homemade," the manager says. "Some guy, big beard, shaggy hair, kept coming in here wanting to sell me balls he'd made. Said if he could get maybe a dozen of them out on a major league field, they'd change the game, big time."

So the manager tells the old guy Sears only buys through their corporate headquarters, but the old timer keeps insisting, so the manager asks how many he can supply, thinking maybe the Sears buyers would be okay with a small quantity of a local product.

Then the old guy says to the manager, "Tell you what. I'll give you one ball. Sell it for whatever you can get for it."

The weird old man pulls a knapsack off his back and draws out a small paperboard box. At this point, the manager waves a hand toward the pyramid, looks back to Grandpa, and says it was just one ball and the old guy wasn't charging for it, so what the hell, and he takes it.

Grandpa thinks this is some new sales gimmick, that maybe there's a catch, and he says, "How come nobody's taken it home?"

A sheepish look from the manager. "You know how baseball folks are, kind of superstitious." Then a chuckle. "You can imagine, can't you, a ball rolling out of that stack would raise the hair on a ball player's neck."

Grandpa shrugs, and the manager looks him up and down and says, "I got to guess you've never played the game."

"Just like to watch," says Grandpa, "but my littlest grandson plays. How much you want for this here ball?"

The manager says, "I'll give it to you, just to get it out of the store."

So Grandpa takes it, catches the trolley, stops at the corner package store with the money he'd planned to use for my present, and he walks into the house with that ball and a bottle of bourbon and some beers, and Mom gives him a mouthful of grief for bringing alcohol into the house. Then she notices the ball.

"What's that?" she says.

He grins. "Well, hell, Shirley, don't you know a baseball when you see one?"

She tells him off again, yells that she might be his daughter but she won't put up with sass from him. Then she takes off on the beer and whiskey again. So they're carrying on like that when Dad drops me off from Boy Scout camp. I open the door, and the whole tiff ceases. I'm excited to see Grandpa, and I don't notice the tension, and I let the screened door bang shut, one more thing that should have set Mom off. But before she can holler at me, Grandpa tosses me the ball. He's more than a little bit looped, and his toss isn't close to being on target. The ball curves leftward and it drops right into my hand as if there was a steel core in the ball and my hand was a magnet. Well, you can believe what you want, but that's what happened. But to go on.

You remember hearing about my Little League team, the Plum Street Pirates, I guess. A lackluster bunch, let me tell you. We didn't even have uniforms. We wore blue jeans and tee shirts with a big "P" cut out of a blue jeans knee patch and ironed on the shirt. Pretty pitiful, huh? Even so, I led the league in homers and strikeouts during both my years as a Pirate. After the first year, I started worrying about the strikeouts, so I'd take a bat and my bag of shag balls to the vacant field over by the train tracks and swat flies. One day I decided to take the ball Grandpa gave me. I pulled it out of the bag, tossed it up, hit the sweet spot just right, and watched, expecting it to go far enough to roll onto the railroad property.

Well, the ball kept on going. It crossed over the ridge the railroad runs on and dropped from sight. Being a brand new ball and a birthday present to boot, I sure didn't want to lose it, so I took off running like mad. I clambered up the ridge to the tracks, and as I started down I began to realize it might've bounced into the pond on that far side. Man! My heart was thumping like mad, because I just knew I'd lost the best ball I'd ever had. I ran though the brush, ripped my jeans on some saw briars, but I kept on going, right to the pond's edge. Sure enough, ripples were still spreading from the middle of the pond. I was about to wade in and hope I could feel the ball with my shoes. Mom was going to be really mad that I'd ruined another pair but I didn't care – I had to have that ball. Then the strangest thing happened. I had my eyes on the center of the ripples, and the water at that point started heaving. The ball bobbed up and started floating toward me.

Say what? It's bullshit? You know, Rick, I considered not telling you this story. I was afraid you'd react this way. All right, why don't we go grab a bite? I know of this pub across town, we can have a couple of brews. But I *am* going to finish the story now that I've started it.

Okay. So after that I go up to Pony League, and I'm finally going to have a uniform. Coach Mack's short of pitchers, and the first day of practice he has three of us take turns throwing batting practice, wanting to see if one of us has pitching potential. I'm the last one to throw. He starts to toss me a ball, but then he notices I'm massaging the ball Grandpa gave me.

"Lemme see that ball, Farmerly," he says, so I hand it to him. He inspects it and then he eyes me. "This ball ain't got no brand."

"It was a birthday present," I tell him. "I think it's homemade."

He looks it over again, picks at the stitches, sniffs, tosses it up a couple of times to check the weight. "All right," he says, "I don't suppose it'd hurt to use this one, seeing as how it's only batting practice." He hands it back.

I'd never used it with other guys around, but now I had no choice, so I nod.

"You know how to throw a curve, Farmerly?" he asks.

Dad, who you'll remember had been a pitcher, wanted me to be one, too, and he had me working on throwing curves, so I say, "And I can throw a forkball, too, Coach. And a slider."

He eyes me skeptically, then says, "Okay, hotshot, let's see what you got."

Kevin Hugenot's next up to take his swings, and he's a real hitter. I decide my first one should be a fastball, right down the middle. If he can't hit that, then I'll have the nerve to try some breaking stuff on him. I rub the ball again, wind up, and throw. Man! It's moving so fast it seems to hop. It hits our catcher Wilton Gibbing's glove with a loud pop. He falls from his crouch, takes off the mitt, rubs his hand, and then tosses me the ball. I straddle the stitches with two fingers and throw my forkball. Kevin swings, and the ball drops like a rock, hits the dirt, takes a crazy bounce, and thuds right into the middle of Wilton's mitt. Kevin mutters something that sounds like sonofabitch. He creeps in, crowds the plate, and I throw a slider. He steps back, thinking he's going to get hit, but the ball whips across the plate and into Wilton's mitt with another big pop.

This time Wilton tosses his mask into the dirt and trots out to me with a look somewhere between irritation and admiration. "What the hell you doing, Karl?" he says, and holds out his glove hand. The palm's swollen and has turned beet red. Then he gives me a pained grin and says, "You break my hand, I'll whip your ass."

I'm about to tell him it's the ball, not me, but he nods toward the next guy up and says, "This guy can't even hit slow breaking stuff, so if you got an off-speed curve, throw a few and give my hand a rest." He trots back, picks up his mask, drops into his crouch, and sets his mitt waist high, right at the middle of the plate. The guy swings once, and I think he might swing again before the ball thunks into Wilton's mitt.

Coach glares at me through the chain link fence in front of the dugout. "Hey," he yells, "lemme see that ball again!"

I trot over. Coach rubs it, hefts it, then puts it in his pocket and throws out another one. What could I do? I throw a fat, juicy serve-up pitch, and the worst batter out there rifles it down the left field line. It curves way foul, bounces on the street, and rolls away. Coach sighs, reaches into his pocket, and tosses me my ball. I motion for Wilton to come out.

"Now what?" he says.

"Your hand can't stand my fast one," I tell him, "and Coach thinks my slow stuff is looking suspicious, so I'm going to throw nothing but medium breaking stuff from now on."

He gives me an odd look, then trots back to the plate, pulls one of those gigantic red handkerchiefs from his pocket, pads the inside of his mitt with it, and motions for me to throw. Well, my breaking stuff's something to see: down, in, out, and always right into Wilton's mitt with a mighty pop.

What? No, thanks, I'll stick to this one Guinness. But you go ahead, have a third if you want. The sandwich and beers are on me, by the way.

So anyway, Coach breaks out a new batch of balls one of the fathers had just brought up, and he tosses me one, tells me to put my ball away. Sure, it's just practice, but the guys light me up like the Fourth of July. Everyone's hitting screamers to the outfield, some of them right through me. But at least it improves everyone's confidence at the plate. After that, Coach puts me on first base for the season opener. After five games, though, I realize I can't hit Pony League pitching and, well, I just quit.

That's right, Rick, I quit. Okay, so you hung in there with the Navy for a quarter of a century, and I changed jobs every other year. So what? You think I'm flaky, right? Well, I might say you were boring all those years, bobbing around on the ocean on those gray-painted Navy bars of soap. Those ships were all you talked about when you came home. As far as I'm concerned, you took the safe path through life, big bro, at least until you got out of the Navy. Me, I took chances my whole working life, and that's why I was able to retire early, why Janice and I have a good, comfortable life now.

Okay, look, Rick, I'm sorry. I didn't mean it. I know you're embarrassed at having to live with us, at having to depend on me to get you to the V.A. Hospital for physical therapy and doctor visits and all that. I don't mind, really I don't.

Well, I guess we'll just have to get used to living under the same roof, won't we?

Anyway, after that, I tried tennis, but I wasn't good enough. I decided to concentrate on my studies, mostly math and science. I stowed the ball in my chest of drawers, went to Western Carolina U. over in Waynesville, and for a long while I never thought about baseball. Then after graduation, when I was working for that first construction outfit, Mom brought a box of mementos to my apartment, and the ball was in there. That started me watching the games on TV. I'd pick the ball up, roll it from hand to hand, juggle it a bit, whatever. All this to say it became a part of my baseball fan experience.

Somewhere in those years, Janice and I married, and for a while family took up most of my free time. But whenever I could, I'd watch Braves games, even the west coast ones. Janice would wake at two in the morning and shuffle downstairs and sit with me for a while before falling asleep on my shoulder.

Then one Saturday morning a couple of years back – Grace was up and out and Leon was just finishing college down at Chapel Hill – Janice started teasing me about baseball. I think maybe because she always saw me watching games with the ball in my hand. It was what she did, Rick. It was an endearment thing, something else you missed out on being a confirmed bachelor.

Anyway, she had this odd look on her face as she sipped her second cup. "You ever think about being involved in baseball again?"

What a question! For years, I'd felt the ball was telling me things, but I can tell by the look on your face that I'd better not go there right now. However it happened, I'd picked up on everything about the game I'd missed out on since Pony League. The signs, how to steal them. How big a lead a runner could take from first base on this pitcher, then that one. I could put myself into any batter's mind, tell you how he was going to approach the coming pitch. I could gauge the effect of wind and temperature on any ball hit. And on and on. I even started a baseball blog, mostly about the Braves, who always seemed to fall off the edge of the earth in the fall run. Over time, I gained a ton of followers, had the most hits on my site of all the b-ball bloggers. Scouts would comment on my posts, would leave these cryptic comments, trying to disguise who they were, I guess. But I knew 'em, I knew 'em all. Most of my regular readers, though, were fans. Everyone who watches the game thinks he has the definitive scoop on the game, the players and such, but I really did. Just about everything I wrote proved out. So, yeah, I told Janice being involved in the game was a constant, nettling thought.

"I want to talk to you about something, then," she said.

I'm sitting there thinking I'm about to pay for another trip to Europe, and she's going to pitch it to me as something I need to get out of what she called my baseball-watching rut.

A pitcher of beer? After those singles? Wow. I haven't seen you drink this much since you got out of the Navy. Your pain medication isn't helping with the hip implant? All that time at sea, and not a scratch, and then you fall off a ladder, at your age. Janice keeps saying you ought to quit house painting, hire some young guys, line up work for 'em. I know, I know, it's hard for me to accept limitations, too. All right, if it'll help with the pain, have at it this time, but I'm taking you back to the V.A. tomorrow. It looks like they botched something with the implant, and I promise you, I'll get some definitive action from your doctor. But back to my story.

So before I can reply, she says, "I know baseball fills a hole in your life, Karl."

There it is. I force a grin so she won't think I'm irritated with her for putting the baseball angle on something she wants. Then she gives me that I-know-something-you-don't smile of hers.

"The Braves," she says, "they've invited you down for spring training."

Talk about being stunned.

"You're going to spring training with the Braves. Florida. Lake Buena Vista."

"I-I don't get it."

"They follow your blog," she says. "Some scout or other told the front office about it, that you have a keen insight into the franchise. They know they never seem to get off to more than a so-so start, that they always have to play catch-up during the season, and what with the pressure, that's probably why they pull an *el foldo* every fall. So some young guy in the front office, a statistician, I think, dug into your blog, tried to call you while you were golfing last week, and then he told the field manager about your blog, who then called the general manager, and they talked. Well, while you were showering this morning, the field manager called, said he and the G.M. want you down there for spring training. They want the team to get off to a flying start, thought someone who knows the players and the game as well as you might offer a needed change of perspective."

At this point I spill what's left of my coffee in my lap. Don't even bother to mop it up. What do you mean what happened? I went down there. Took my baseball with me. No, of course I didn't pitch any, and I didn't hit, either. They took me to the press box and put a mic on me that sent a signal to an earpiece the field manager was wearing. He'd told me to treat infield practice, batting practice and the like, as if I were watching TV at home, just make my usual comments.

Well, everything went great for a couple of weeks. The team really seemed to shape up. The infield guys were handling the ball like they were the Harlem Globetrotters. Hitters were taking good, clean cuts. Pitchers had amazing stuff. And then the exhibition games started. They still wanted me there, alone and high up in the stands, so the press and scouts wouldn't pick up on what I was doing, and I kept making my comments.

Then came the fifth game, against the Cards. A rookie comes to bat, a guy the Braves had called up from their team in the Carolina League, a strapping, tattooed, shaved-head first baseman. I tell the manager over the mic that this pitcher for the Cards, also a rookie, is no doubt going to start with a heater down the chute, because he hates getting behind in the count. The manager goes though his signs, the third base coach goes through his, and the batter nods. He swings.

And that's when something goes wrong. He crushes the ball to straightaway center the way I'd expected, but the ball keeps going, is still rising as it passes over the scoreboard. I'd gained a feel for how far each batter should be able to hit the ball, had watched this guy bounce a few off the scoreboard, but this homer is way out of kilter. Several minutes later, the announcer says some kid had been outside the park near centerfield, had seen the ball land, had brought it back to the ball park, and from what he'd told the park officials, the ball had traveled well over six hundred feet. Unbelievable! And here's something else I should tell you. Whenever I'd pick up the ball, it'd be warm, warmer than my hand, as if it'd been in play on a hot day.

Well, how the ball felt *was* a big deal, Rick, at least for me. By now you know how I was about it, right? I was convinced it was alive, that besides giving its owner a lot of baseball skill on the field, it held some phantom baseball intelligence and would impart its knowledge to whomever owned the ball. So at the moment the rookie hit that stupendous dinger, I was holding the ball, even juggling it a bit as I watched. That was my way of working with it. It would communicate with me casually, as an old friend might.

How? With subtle feelings, I guess you can say. Jeez, Rick, you're so linear in your thinking. I mean, who cares how?

Anyway, about the time that dinger reached the point at which it should have started falling, I dropped my ball. I picked it up, and it was cold, like a rock on a winter day. I *knew* then. The ball *had* been alive, all right, and like all living things its life had a beginning and an end. My ball had never taken on much of a role on the playing field, but in its middle and later years it had found a way to share a storehouse of baseball knowledge with those on the field. But like all living things, it died. I think now that when our time draws near, most of us go quietly, maybe too quietly. But there's always an element of drama to anything associated with baseball, and I honestly believe that as this ball's life force soared heavenward, it attached itself to that rookie's homer. My thinking is that it wanted to allow itself one last, grand, major league ride, going out with a bang instead of a whimper.

I kept holding the ball, but of course nothing came. Where I used to be on top of everything, after that dinger I didn't seem to know a thing about baseball. Not a flipping thing. I tried to make a few comments to the field manager, but what I was saying didn't make sense. He asked me what the hell was going on. I didn't know what else to tell him, so I simply said I didn't have anything else to contribute. He didn't say a word for a while. Then he told me to take off the mic and come sit with him in the dugout. I did, and we talked about that day's game. Players came over, signed a program for me, and I had a great time.

So why have I kept the ball? Don't you see, Rick? We gave the best parts of our lives to the Navy and the construction business. We didn't contribute a lot, I guess, but we did what we were capable of. All because Mom and Dad, and even Grandpa, sacrificed so our lives could be what we could make of them. I keep the ball and toy with it for the same reason we visit Mom and Dad's graves every spring, why they kept Grandpa's ashes in an urn in the hall. It's good to honor a life, for all the ways it's made ours better. This ball did that for me, bro. And for a little while it did that for the game.

ABOUT THE AUTHOR

Bob Mustin has had a brief naval career and a longer one as a civil engineer, and has been a North Carolina Writers Network writer-in-residence at Peace College under the late Doris Betts' guiding hand. In the early '90s, he was the editor of a small literary journal, The Rural Sophisticate, based in Georgia. His work has appeared in The Rockhurst Review, Elysian Fields Quarterly, Cooweescoowee, Under the Sun, Gihon River Review, Reflections Literary Journal, and many sites in electronic form.

To Learn More about Bob Mustin, visit:

Website: www.BobMustin.com

Blog: Bobmust.wordpress.com

ACKNOWLEDGMENTS

No book, no story, no sentence, is the rightful domain of the author alone, and that's all too true of this collection. I have to thank Mike Aloisi for his continuing commitment to my writing. And I also want to thank Paul Michael Anderson, a curmudgeon at too young an age, for his thoughtful editing, and to thank Giants fanatic Dave Frauenfelder for his occasional exclamations regarding baseball, which lead me to write about that sport, and to the judges of the Annual Appalachian Authors Guild Fiction Competition for their recognition of work included here.

RECOGNITION

"The Object of Affection" was published on the web on TheSquareTable.com, Fall 2005 issue.

"The Offering" was published in Torn Realities Anthology, Post Mortem Press, 2012.

"I, Singularity" won the 2013 Annual Fiction Award from the Appalachian Authors Guild.